Delicious
Temptation

a Delicious Desires novel

Sabrina Sol

Entangled Publishing, LLC
2614 South Timberline Road
Suite 109
Fort Collins, CO 80525
Visit our website at www.entangledpublishing.com.

Brazen is an imprint of Entangled Publishing, LLC. For more information on our titles, visit www.brazenbooks.com.

Edited by Heather Howland
Cover design by Heather Howland
Cover art by Depositphotos

Manufactured in the United States of America

First Edition May 2015

For Louisa Bacio, Nikki Prince and Elizabeth Scott for always believing that I could.

Chapter One

Death by cupcake.

In the grand scheme of things, Amara could think of worse ways to go. Although technically it would be "death by watching someone *else* eat a cupcake." Not as exciting. And probably not even possible.

While watching her parents carefully nibble at the *tres leches* cupcake she'd baked might not kill her, it could definitely drive her to the brink of insanity. How long did it take to eat a cupcake, anyway? Her dad could gobble up an entire lemon meringue pie in the blink of an eye—if her mother wasn't around to stop him.

No, she knew them too well. Their slow and deliberate chewing was a delay tactic—a trick to prevent them from having to deliver bad news for as long as possible. She'd gotten wise to their ways over the twenty-six years of her life.

She couldn't take it anymore. "Well? What do you think?"

Her parents looked at each other and then at the half-eaten cupcake in her dad's hand.

He cleared his throat. "It's mois—"

"Don't say it. You know I hate that word," her mom warned.

He popped the last of the cupcake into his mouth and mumbled, "*Que*? Moist?"

"Aaaah! You said it!" Her mom threw her hands up in the air. "Ricardo, why did you say it when I told you not to say it?"

"*Calmate vieja*!"

Amara winced. Her dad was in for it now. No one called her mom an old woman. No one.

If she weren't so irritated by their evasive tactics, Amara might have laughed. Her parents' bickering escalated into full-blown Spanish, complete with her mom's usual dramatic gesturing. She sighed, picked up a cupcake, and took a huge bite. It *was* moist. The airy sponge cake texture had beautifully absorbed the combination of evaporated milk, sweetened condensed milk, and coconut milk, filling each nook and cranny with little bubbles of sweetness. She licked the coconut cream frosting from her fingers. Decadent and smooth, with a hint of vanilla and rum. Not bad. But something was missing.

Amara reviewed the recipe in her head, searching for something she might have done wrong. Too much coconut milk or not enough? Maybe she should have baked them a minute more. Or maybe it was the frosting—was the rum too overpowering?

She forced herself to stop dissecting the dessert. Deep down she knew more or less rum wasn't going to make a difference. No one but her parents and she would ever taste these cupcakes anyway. She picked up the last two from the tray and readied herself for the speech she'd heard a million times before.

That is, if they ever stopped arguing with each other.

"Hello?" she tried. When that didn't quiet them, she yelled, "Mom! Dad! Enough!"

Silence. Her parents turned to look at her. "Amara Maria Robles, there is no need to scream at me," her mother huffed.

"I'm sorry, Mom. I was trying to get you two to stop arguing."

"Aye, *mija*, we weren't arguing. We were….how you say? Discussing," her father said.

"Fine, then can you stop discussing for a second, and tell me what you think of my cupcakes?"

"Well, I think they are very…" He stole a glance at her mother. "…good. Yes, very good. But…."

And here it comes.

Her mother walked over and hooked her arm around Amara's waist. "It's just that cupcakes are usually for children, but children don't always like *tres leches*. You know this. Our orders for *tres leches* cakes are usually for weddings or anniversaries. *Los chiquillos*, they like chocolate or strawberry with pictures of that weird sponge boy or Dora the Explorer on the tops. That's what the children like." She emphasized the last part by squeezing Amara's waist a little tighter. "Even you had to go all the way to Chicago before you would try a *tres leches* cake, remember?"

Of course she remembered. She remembered everything about Chicago, especially the day she found out that she'd made the short list to become the next head pastry chef at the posh Lakeside Resort & Spa. It was the same day her mother had called, begging Amara through tears to come back to East Los Angeles and help run the bakery. So, like a good daughter, she'd given her notice at the resort and moved back home within a matter of weeks.

"Besides," her mother added, raising an eyebrow. "I thought you were done with the silly cupcake ideas? Or did you already forget what happened the last time?"

She unhooked herself from her mother's grip and walked toward the silver trashcan in the corner. She'd rather sacrifice her cupcakes than have another conversation about *the last time*. Her mother knew very well that Amara hadn't forgotten. How could she, when they brought it up when-ever they wanted to prove, yet again, that her parents knew what was best?

"Hey, hey, hey, don't throw them away." Her father plucked the cupcakes from her hands before Amara could toss them. "I said I liked them."

Just as he was about to take a bite into one, her mother stole them both right out of his hands. "Uh, uh. You already had one. No more today, Mr. Diabetes." Then she dumped them into the garbage.

Ouch.

Even though Amara had planned to throw them away herself, it hurt to see her mother do it without a second thought.

Her father walked over to her and kissed her forehead. "They were good cupcakes, very good. They were just too, how you say? Gourmet."

Her mother gestured around the small space, as if the

chipped Formica counter, worn linoleum floor, and display cases that were older than Amara were the answer to everything. "East L.A. isn't Chicago, and the Robles Panaderia isn't like the fancy hotel where you used to work. Our customers expect the same simple and traditional recipes we've been selling for almost thirty years. Deep down, I think you know that it's best just to give people what they expect." She poked through her purse, looking for God knows what, then produced their pharmacy card. "Don't forget to pull the next batch of *orejas* out of the oven while we pick up your father's medicines. If you leave them in too long the sugar burns the puff pastry. Okay?"

Amara nodded, even though it wasn't okay. They'd insisted she come home to help save the bakery, but in the end, they hadn't wanted help at all. How many times had they shot down her ideas for how to freshen up the menu to bring in new customers?

She sighed. Their unyielding grip on "simple and traditional" would probably be the end of the business they had worked so hard to build.

But rather than tell them that, Amara picked at the sprinkle of crumbs left behind on the counter—the only edible reminder of her "too gourmet" *tres leches* cupcakes with coconut cream frosting.

As her parents walked through the bakery's kitchen toward the back exit, she heard her father tell her mother, "Consuelo, why are you always so hard on her? She wants to help. She's a good daughter, a good—" The thick wooden door slammed on the rest of his sentence, but it didn't matter. They were the words she'd heard all her life.

She's a good girl.

Amara grabbed the Windex and the roll of paper towels from underneath the cash register and wiped down the display case. Again. Dome-shaped sweet breads with a chocolate crumbly checkerboard topping, nut-covered pound cakes, cinnamon and sugar dusted *churros*, pink shortbread cookies, and custard-filled pastries looked back at her through the clean glass. "That's me, all right. Good, nice, sweet. I might as well be one of these freaking cream puffs," she announced to the empty store.

A low buzzing sound answered her back, reminding her that the *orejas* were still in the oven.

She turned to head into the kitchen, but the jingle of the front door opening made her turn back again.

At first she only saw a black L.A. Dodgers baseball cap entering the bakery. It cast a shadow over a squared jaw covered with dark stubble. A black T-shirt clung to broad shoulders and a flat chest. Her eyes dropped to formfitting, faded blue jeans with an unmistakable bulge in the center.

Amara inhaled sharply and coughed. "Can I help you?" she managed to sputter out after a few seconds.

The mystery man took off his baseball cap and walked up to the counter. "I sure hope so," he said, and flashed a smile made for sinning. "I'm looking for Miguel Robles."

Familiar brown eyes stared into hers. Even after twelve years, she recognized those lush, thick eyelashes in an instant.

Eric.

Her chest tightened. Her fingers gripped the counter. Her voice caught in her throat. Typical reaction when you've seen a ghost. Especially a ghost who'd just zapped every part of your body back to life. She still didn't make a sound. Couldn't.

He continued, "My name is Eric Valencia. Miguel and I are, well, we used to be…we went to high school together." He squinted at her with those beautiful, dark eyes. "His family still owns this bakery, right?"

Amara nodded.

"Okay. Good. Can I leave something for him?"

Again, a nod.

He dug into his back pocket and pulled out a folded white envelope and handed it to her. "This is a letter for Miguel. Please make sure he gets it. If he decides he wants to reach me, you can tell him I'm staying at my *abuela*'s house. My cell number's on the letter, too."

She reached for the envelope, and her fingers brushed his as she took it from him. The contact warmed her from the inside out. After shoving the letter into the top center pocket of her full apron, she tried to nonchalantly wipe her sweaty palms on the sides of her jeans. Amara expected her surprise visitor to leave at that point, but he didn't budge. And the longer he stood there staring at her, the warmer she got, especially, in one particular area of her body.

Then he unleashed his infamous roguish smirk. The one that let you know he was the sort who regularly thought wicked things and was now thinking them about you. "So, I've told you my name. Are you going to tell me yours?"

The fact that he didn't recognize her shouldn't have wounded her, but it did. She'd known him since he was nine years old and became her brother Miguel's best friend in the fourth grade. Maybe she should be happy he didn't automatically see the chubby little girl who used to beg to borrow his CDs, or bake him special batches of chocolate chip cookies. She was fourteen the last time she'd seen him. But had twelve years really changed her that much?

She wondered how she must look to him now and followed his flirty gaze. It moved from her eyes to her lips to below her neck and she swore she felt it. His eyes continued downward and lingered there longer than appropriate. Amara looked down and saw her D-cup cleavage now prominently on display, like the bakery's selection of treats. Warmth spread to her cheeks and neck as she realized she'd accidentally pushed down the front of her pink V-neck T-shirt when she'd shoved his letter into her apron. Even more embarrassing? The tops of her breasts looked as if they were being squeezed from the clutches of her cheeky-turned-ironic "I Like It Spicy" black apron.

Ah. No wonder he didn't recognize her right away. She didn't have those at fourteen. Adjusting her position against the counter, Amara pulled up her apron. That did the trick and his trance broke.

Eric's smoldering, yet also appreciative, stare found its way back to her face. "You look familiar. Did you go to Roosevelt?"

"I did. But I wasn't in your class." She'd been a lowly freshman when Eric and Miguel had been seniors.

"Maybe we passed each other in the halls, then? Although, I'm sure I would've stopped to talk to someone as pretty as you."

Before she could rein it in, a silly giggle escaped her throat but it stopped as soon as he took one of her hands and said, "I would say it was very nice to meet you. But I still don't know your name." His touch ignited a backdraft of arousal that swooshed through her body, and a heat exploded between them, which he acknowledged with a slow, confident smile. Her body was so turned on, so hot that she thought she smelled smoke.

That's because you're playing with fire.

Eric Valencia had been Roosevelt High's resident bad boy. Trouble followed him wherever he went. And so did the girls. It frustrated her parents to no end that Miguel insisted on staying friends with him, especially when they were seniors and that trouble started to involve drinking and run-ins with the police. Back then, even Amara knew that Eric wasn't the type of guy you ended up marrying. No, he was the one you ended up screwing just to piss off your boyfriend or parents.

Her mom *had* made her pretty mad this morning…

Despite this burning need to know what it felt like to be just a little bit bad with a bad boy like Eric, Amara decided to tell him her name, even if meant dousing the sparks between them. "You probably won't believe me, but my name is…."

Wait. She really did smell smoke. The *orejas*!

Amara snatched her hand away, ran to the kitchen, and discovered it engulfed in a sooty gray cloud. She turned off the oven. On cue, the smoke detector began wailing. She yanked open the oven door. Even more smoke poured out. "Oh my gosh, oh my gosh, oh my gosh." Frantically, she searched for her potholders but couldn't find them fast enough.

"Stand back." A deep voice cut through the haze. Eric grabbed a dishtowel from the counter and reached for the baking sheet filled with blackened ear-shaped pastries. Before she could tell him the dishtowel was way too thin to protect his fingers, he pulled the *orejas* out of the oven.

"Son of a bitch!" The tray crashed to the ground. The

pieces that weren't stuck to the bottom of the pan scattered across the tile floor like charred pebbles. Eric continued swearing as he waved his injured hand.

Amara rushed over. "Oh my gosh! Is it bad? Let me see." She pulled his arm down to examine the damage. Red blisters were starting to form on the pads of his right index finger and thumb. "Come over here so I can run some cold water over your fingers," she said while pulling him by his non-burned hand in the direction of the stainless steel sink. "Hopefully that will take some of the sting away."

He let her guide him through the kitchen, and she flipped on the faucet and gently pulled his hand under the water. "Okay, stay here and I'll be right back." Amara went to the pantry and grabbed a broom. After positioning herself directly underneath the smoke detector on the ceiling, she lifted the broom's handle and maneuvered it until she could push the "off" button. The incessant beeping stopped.

"Thank God," Eric shouted as she put the broom away. "My poor ears. I think they hurt more than the burns on my fingers."

When he laughed, Amara smiled in her heart. She used to live to make him laugh.

Stop it. You're not fourteen, and he's not your brother's best friend anymore. He's basically a stranger.

Time to get him out of there and clean up the mess before her parents came back. "Any better? Is the water helping?"

He showed her his fingers. "The pain is better, but I bet these blisters won't go away anytime soon." He faced her now, his back against the sink.

"I've got just the cure for that." She reached over his

shoulder to grab the plant sitting on the windowsill behind him.

"Are you going to kiss it and make it better?" he asked, his voice low and husky.

She made a note that he'd gotten more forward since he'd been away. Or maybe it was because she'd never been on the receiving end of his flirtation? Either way, she wasn't sure how to handle this dangerous dance. His breath fanned her hair and she willed herself not to turn her head. Because one look into those dark, sexy eyes would surely cause her lady parts to burst into flames and set the smoke detector off all over again.

"What? No. I meant I have this." She showed him the plant. "It's aloe vera. It'll help with the blisters."

"If you say so. But I still may need that kiss. You know, just in case," he said with a wink.

The fact that he could flirt despite his obvious pain both surprised and flattered her. She brushed it off. She didn't practice the art of flirting on a regular basis. She had no sexy comeback. No feminine wiles to bring him to his knees. Not that she wanted him on his knees or in any other suggestive position. Maybe. So she focused on doing what she *did* know—fixing what needed to be fixed.

Amara grabbed a pair of kitchen scissors from a nearby drawer, trimmed a thick leaf off the plant, and cut it into two. She squeezed until little droplets of its soothing juice appeared. "Okay, give me your hand."

Eric obeyed, and she held it carefully and rubbed the exposed plant end across his fingers. He jerked.

She stopped and looked at him. "I'm sorry. I don't want to hurt you."

He met her stare. "You're not hurting me. In fact, you're having kind of an opposite effect on me."

Amara dropped her eyes and continued her first aid. "That's the aloe vera talking. You're lucky. If my *abuela* were here, she'd be rubbing mustard all over your hand."

"Ha! Mine would be sticking my fingers into a tub of butter. Sounds like maybe our grandmothers should get together and exchange home remedies."

She smiled but didn't laugh. "My *abuela* passed away a few years ago."

"I'm sorry about that." Eric raised his non-injured hand and lifted her chin with one finger. "Thank you for taking such good care of me. I hope the Robles family knows how lucky they are to have you."

Amara's heart raced. He stared at her, and this time she couldn't look away if she tried. The want and need she saw reflected in the dark pools of his eyes reeled her in. Eric Valencia—the object of her silly teenage girl crush and regular subject of her grown woman fantasies—wanted to kiss her. And at that moment, she wanted nothing more in this world than to kiss him back.

It shocked the heck out of her that she was actually admitting it. What would people—what would her parents—say if they knew good girl Amara was thinking of making out with some man in the bakery's kitchen? Although Eric wasn't just *some man,* and that made it even more scandalous. The *chisme* police would have a field day.

Who says they have to know?

She'd given up so much over the years in order to do what she was told or what was expected. Stealing one kiss—one small piece of pleasure for herself—wasn't only justified, it was well deserved.

And the fact that it was Eric gave it a certain forbidden feel that made it all the more tempting. It didn't even matter that he'd just walked back into her life. The want she knew as a teenager had flared into raging desire the moment she'd recognized him.

So when he finally slid one arm around her waist to pull her closer, she didn't stop him. He tipped her chin upward and she closed her eyes as their lips brushed against each other for one soft, hesitant first kiss. The contact lasted only a few seconds. Just long enough to make her crave a second one. Her eyes opened and she met his questioning gaze. He looked at Amara as if she'd appeared out of thin air and he had no idea how his mouth had ended up on hers.

Before panicky thoughts could set in about whether his puzzled expression meant he regretted the kiss, large calloused hands framed her face and his lips found hers one more time.

The gentleness from before vanished. This kiss was hard and deep.

His tongue pressed at her mouth, demanding she open for him. She surrendered willingly, clutching his shoulders for support as her body gave way against his. Her small cries of pleasure elicited deep, throaty groans from him. He moved his hands from her face to roam across her body in desperate exploration until finally cradling her back as he pulled her into a full embrace.

Everything else fell away at that moment. She lost herself in him and the way he kissed her. She'd been kissed before, of course. But never like this.

Fevered. Unrestrained. Shameless.

Every nerve and every one of her senses zinged to life. And with every kiss, he recharged her soul. It was exactly what she'd needed after that morning. She felt reckless and wild—the antithesis of every thing she'd ever been taught to be.

And she loved it. Especially what he was doing at that exact moment with his tongue to the curve of her neck.

Except for a small wince of pain when he grabbed her by the waist and lifted her onto the countertop by the sink, it seemed as if Eric had forgotten all about his burned fingers. And when he wedged himself between her thighs, so did she. Ohmigod. The feel of him growing harder by the second, right where she'd always dreamed of having him, sent Amara's body into overload. Her heart rate sped up, her body quivered, and her breathing…well, who needed to breathe anyway. She clawed at his shirt, desperate to get closer.

But when his hand slid under the front of her apron and she felt his thumb brush the skin behind the buttons of her jeans, it triggered her internal alarm bell of sensibility. Although she wanted what was happening, the conventional side of her couldn't let things go any further until he knew who she really was.

"Wait," she whispered, placing an open palm against his hard chest. "I have to tell you something."

His brows furrowed into a question.

She opened her mouth as the front door of the bakery jingled.

"Amara, it's me! Your dad left his wallet by the cash register. I swear that man does things just to make me crazy."

She vaulted off the counter and shot a glance at Eric.

Recognition crossed his face like a wave crashing onto

the beach, changing everything that had been there before. "Amara?" He looked at her from head to toe and back again. Shock—perhaps even disappointment—replaced the desire in his eyes, and he stepped back. *Way* back.

"How come something smells like it's burning. *Aye dios*, what happened here?" Her mother stood in the doorway, and by her contorted expression, Amara knew she'd be explaining this for days.

"The *orejas* burned and I couldn't find the potholders, so Eric grabbed the pan with a dishtowel, but it was too hot, so he had to drop the pan, and he burned his fingers, so I was putting aloe vera on him... I mean, on his blisters."

"Eric? Eric Valencia?" When Consuelo's laser stare moved to the man standing next to her, Amara swore the temperature in the kitchen dropped a few degrees. She took a slight step away from him.

"Yes, it's me. So good to see you, *Señora* Robles." Eric moved as if he were about to hug her mom, but then stopped. He folded and unfolded his arms nervously across his chest.

Amara tried not to smirk, especially since her mother had *that* look on her face.

"Wow, what's it been? Twelve years? What brings you back here?"

"Different things," he answered, glancing at Amara. "I actually came today to try to find Miguel."

Her mom bent to pick up the baking sheet from the floor. She carried it toward the sink, walking between Amara and Eric and forcing them to move even farther away from each other. She dropped the pan into the sink with a loud clatter that reverberated throughout the room. When it was quiet, she addressed Eric. "My Miguel works as an architect for a very successful firm downtown. He doesn't really come by the bakery during the week. We'll make sure to tell him you stopped by, though." The sweetness of her tone was as fake as the saccharine her dad put in his *café con leche*.

"Thank you. I would appreciate it. In fact, I already gave my number to your daughter."

Consuelo glared at her.

"I'd better be going then. It was so very nice meeting you, I mean *seeing* you again, Amara," he said, emphasizing her name by rolling the "r." "*Buenas tardes, Señora* Robles.*"* Then he strolled out of the kitchen to the front of the bakery.

Jingle. Jingle.

Her mom held out her hand. "Give me the number."

"But, Mom, don't you think it should be up to Miguel if he wants to call him or not?"

"*Dámelo.* Now."

She reached into her apron pocket and gave the envelope to her mother, who then proceeded to throw it in the trash.

"That boy should never have come back here. He's always been trouble and was always trying to get your brother into trouble with him. As far as I'm concerned, Miguel does not need to be friends with Eric Valencia again." Consuelo walked to the pantry to retrieve the broom. Handing it to Amara, she said, "I thank the Virgin Mary every night that he never tried any funny business with you. It's like I always tell you, *mija.* Girls like you don't need to bother with boys like him. They take what they want and then disappear, leaving you and everyone else to clean up their mess." She pointed to the floor and walked out.

As Amara swept up the pieces of burnt pastry, she tried to push any thoughts of Eric out of her mind. Her mother was probably right—neither she nor Miguel needed the complication that was Eric back in their lives.

Dear Lord, did she really just admit that her mother was *right*?

She walked over to empty the dustpan into the trash and spotted Eric's envelope lying neatly on top of some wadded-up paper towels.

The warmth of his touch came rushing back, along with the aching desire he'd awakened, and she couldn't help but brush her lips with her fingers as she remembered how good it had felt to be bad.

She looked around the empty kitchen, took a deep breath, and reached into the trash.

Chapter Two

Amara Robles.

Eric stood outside the bakery, still not quite believing what had just happened. If it weren't for the throbbing blisters on his fingers he might have convinced himself it had been nothing more than an alcohol-induced hallucination. But he wasn't drunk—hadn't been drunk in more than eighteen months.

He'd been stone cold sober when he hit on his ex-best friend's little sister. Stone cold sober when he'd kissed her full, sweet lips and slipped his hand underneath her jeans to feel her smooth skin. Thankfully his hard-on had disappeared as soon as Amara's mother showed up. But he could still feel the lust deep in his bones. He needed to walk it off before those feelings traveled south and made walking the two blocks home very difficult indeed.

I better take the long way back.

As he made his way past the colorful stucco houses

crammed side by side along the hilly neighborhoods of East Los Angeles, Eric couldn't help remembering all the times he and Miguel walked this very route to get to each other's homes. Just as the Robles' bakery still stood at the same Eastern Avenue location it had when he was a teen, the family's bright peach-colored ranch style house also still sat in the same place—across the street from the bakery and just around the corner on Marney Street. A lifetime ago, Eric and his mom had lived on Marney, too.

The neighborhood hadn't changed much, but Amara sure had. It'd been pure physical attraction that had made him start to flirt with her in the first place. Although she'd looked familiar, no way did the thought ever cross his mind that the sexy woman behind the counter was none other than Miguel's little sister. For starters, last he heard, she'd moved away and got a job as a chef somewhere. So why was she back? And when had this transformation of hers taken place?

When he'd left East L.A., Amara had just been a silly teenage girl, but now she was definitely all woman. Grown-up Amara had curves in all of the right places. Curves a man could get lost in. His cock stirred under his tight jeans as he thought about the teasing glimpse he'd caught of those ample breasts, her nails digging into his skin through the thin material of his T-shirt, and the feel of her thighs wrapped around his own. He'd never be able to forget that her hair smelled of shampoo and cinnamon, that her tongue tasted like mint, or that her eyes had begged him after that first kiss to take more from her.

And so he had.

Who knew how much further things would've gone if her mother hadn't shown up? He was halfway to thrusting into her, for fuck's sake.

If he had known her true identity at first, he would've thanked her for taking care of his injury and then headed straight for the door. No matter how good she'd tasted, or felt in his arms, Amara was off limits. And not just because she was a Robles, but because she deserved better than him and the rough, frantic way he'd manhandled her at the bakery. No wonder she'd pulled away once he tried to do more than just kiss her.

The fact that she had kept on kissing him despite knowing who *he* was surprised him, though. Not that he'd ever had a problem with girls wanting to kiss him. Or any trouble earning his fuck 'em and leave 'em reputation with those same girls. He knew that afterward, they always whispered to their friends about how they'd been bad with Eric Valencia and how lucky they were that he hadn't burned them in the process. He'd learned to shrug them off and not care what they said or who they told. After all, they knew perfectly well what it meant to hook up with him.

Nothing.

Turned out, though, whispers didn't go away no matter how old you got.

Ever since returning to the old neighborhood a few weeks ago, he'd heard them as he left the grocery store or entered the taco shop on the corner. It was mainly older women or teenage girls, sending each other knowing looks and hiding their mouths behind their animated hands.

Even after all these years, this tight-knit Catholic community wouldn't let him forget the sins of his past. He admitted he'd been a punk back in the day—tagging buildings, ditching school, shoplifting whatever he could from the corner liquor store. One time he'd even convinced Miguel to help him steal tools from a neighbor's garage. They'd gotten caught and Miguel's dad had to pay the neighbor off so he wouldn't call the police.

Eric's mom used to tell him if he didn't straighten up he'd end up just like his own dad—a drunk who got knifed during a bar fight when Eric was just two years old. But it wasn't until Eric's high school girlfriend got pregnant just weeks before graduation that he decided to quit drinking and started thinking about making something of his life. He let himself believe he could be a regular guy with a steady job and a wife and kids at home.

Then she'd miscarried and everything changed again.

He tried to shake off the memories as he walked up the steps to his home.

It still felt weird to call the small blue house on Drucker Street "home." For as long as he could remember, he'd known it as "*abuela's* house." But now he lived there, too, in the shadow of the Cal State Los Angeles campus. Even back in high school he knew he'd never be a student there. Guys like him didn't do college. No, he'd always been destined for a harder life. Ironically, the only reason he didn't end up in a gang was because he didn't do well following orders. It didn't matter in the end. Everything still went to shit.

The rich, mouthwatering aroma of beef soup greeted him as soon as he walked through the door. His stomach grumbled, even though he'd eaten a breakfast burrito only a few hours earlier. He'd already gained a few pounds since coming back—something his *abuela* took much delight in. When he showed up on her doorstep two weeks ago, she nearly cried. Not because she was happy to see him, but because he was so skinny. She fed him nonstop that first day, and he loved it.

"It smells so good in here," he told her as he walked into the kitchen. He found her sitting at the table chopping cilantro. "I love your *cocido*."

He bent down to kiss her cheek and she smiled. "Makes me happy to cook it for you, *mijo*. It's ready. Let me serve you."

"*Mamá*, he's almost thirty years old. He can get his own food," Eric's mother yelled from the bathroom down the hallway. His *abuela* waved her hand in his mother's direction and started to get up from her chair.

"She's right. I can get it myself, and I'll get yours, too." He kissed her cheek again and walked to the cupboard to grab two bowls.

"Did you get the *tortillas*?" his mother asked as she entered the kitchen.

Damn it.

"I forgot." He didn't need to turn around to see her disappointment—it was the only look she gave him these days.

"Just take the bread for sandwiches, Diana. *Es lo mismo*," his *abuela* said.

"It's not the same, *Mamá*. That's why you asked him to go to the bakery in the first place. You were the one who wanted the *tortillas*," his mom said. "I swear it's like you have amnesia when it comes to him."

Eric put his bowl down. It was too early for a fight. "I can go to the liquor store on the corner and be back before you have to leave." No way was he going back to the Robles Bakery. At least not today.

"Forget it, Eric. I'll take the bread. I need to leave a little early anyway so I can pick up Frances from the bus stop." She poured herself some soup in a round plastic container and shoved it into her insulated lunch bag. After grabbing a water bottle and a piece of bread, she kissed his *abuela* good-bye.

"Remember, I'll be home by eight-thirty tonight," she said to him. "She already had her aspirin this morning so just make sure she takes the heart pill and cholesterol pill after the first *novela* ends and before the second starts. Otherwise she'll fall asleep and not take any of them."

He nodded between slurps. It was the same routine he'd followed for the past fourteen days. He knew what to do to take care of his *abuela*, but he accepted the fact that his mother still had to tell him. After all, he'd agreed to live there under her terms.

After his mom left, he looked at his *abuela* and winked. She just shook her head and sighed. They both went back to eating their soup.

"*Abuela*, if you really want *tortillas* I can still go to the store."

"Eh, *es* okay, *mijo*. I don't need them after all."

"I'm sorry I forgot them. It's just that I got there and I was, um, distracted." *In more ways than one.*

"Did you find your friend?"

"No, he wasn't there. But I talked to his mother...and his sister."

"Oh, yes, Amara. She works there now. Such a nice girl."

It killed him to not ask for more information, but his *abuela* was smart. And far too nosy. He'd have to bide his time and ask when she wouldn't be likely to suspect his motives. He finished his soup, thoughts of the shy, awkward tomboy who'd turned into such a desirable woman spinning through his head.

After he'd cleaned the kitchen, Eric pulled out a deck of cards from one of the cabinet drawers. He needed more information, and his grandma *loved* to gossip while playing solitaire.

He waited until she dealt out her hand before starting the interrogation. "So do you know why Amara is working at the bakery? You told me last year that she moved to Chicago."

His grandma studied the cards. "She come back a few months ago. Ricardo hurt his back trying to pull something off a shelf. Then the doctor tell him he has the diabetes and high blood pressure and that he needs to stop working so much. *Pues*, Miguel has his own job and a wife—you know he married that girl you went to school with and she's pregnant now... Aha! I won!"

He waited patiently until she dealt herself another round of cards and tried to get her back to the story. "So did Señor Robles tell Amara she had to quit and come home?" Although he couldn't explain why, the thought turned his stomach.

His *abuela* shrugged. "*No se*, but she's a good daughter. I'm sure she would do anything to help her family. Especially now."

That didn't sound good. "What do you mean especially now, *abuela*?"

"Oh, yes, well, the bakery isn't as busy as it used to be. Poor Consuelo told Father Marco that they might close soon if they don't get more business. She even asked Father Marco if they could start selling their *pan dulce* from a cart after Sunday Mass. He told her that the youth group already does that to raise money for their trips. She almost cried, that poor lady."

As his *abuela* played two more rounds of solitaire, Eric absorbed the information. The Robles' family business was in trouble, and Amara had been summoned to fix it. That was a lot of responsibility to bear on such beautiful shoulders.

Eric shook his head, clearing the memory of her soft cries against his lips from his mind. *Forget about her.* He hadn't come back home to fuck his ex-best friend's sister, no matter how tempting the thought might be. He'd come back for a chance to start his life over and prove to himself and to others that he could be more than just a drunk or a criminal. He needed to concentrate on taking care of his *abuela* and getting back on his feet financially so he could rebuild his construction company. He also needed to make things right with Miguel—probably the only person in the world who had put up with all of his bullshit, no matter what, and Eric had basically repaid him by disappearing for twelve years. That was why he'd written the letter. He had to apologize and let Miguel know why he'd left and why he'd stayed away for so long.

Tarnishing his little sister's reputation with a meaningless one-night stand probably wasn't going to win Eric any bonus points.

He had to stop thinking of Amara as the sexy woman he'd just made out with. In fact, it would be better for them both if he just stopped thinking of her altogether, since he was pretty sure she'd come to her senses and regret ever having kissed him.

Chapter Three

"Ugh, I'm going to gain fifty pounds by the end of the week. Why couldn't your parents own a beet farm instead of a bakery? I hate beets."

Amara looked at her cousin Daisy, who had just finished stuffing a cheese-filled Danish into her mouth.

"Maybe you should try selling the stuff instead of eating it?"

Daisy wiped her bright-red lips with a napkin. "And who exactly am I supposed to be selling it to? We haven't had a customer in over an hour."

"I know. Friday is usually one of our busiest days. I'm sure we'll get a rush around lunchtime," Amara said as she put on a new pot of coffee to brew. Truth was, she wasn't sure at all. The weekends were getting to be almost as slow as the weekdays, and that was beyond worrisome. That's why she'd enlisted her cousin's help. She needed some fresh ideas and a plan to get new customers in the door.

Daisy and her expensive college marketing degree had been "let go" from her agency last month. Only Amara knew that she'd really quit after getting into it with her boss—again. Her dad would've been furious if he knew, especially since he was still helping her pay off her student loans. Daisy told everyone she'd been laid off and moved back home. But just like his brother, Carlos Robles didn't believe in free rides. He'd given her six months to find a job at another agency or else he'd get her a job himself at the factory where he worked. Daisy had agreed to his terms, but confided to Amara that although she didn't want to work at another agency, or at the factory, she had no idea what she *did* want to do. So Amara convinced her to help out at the bakery until she figured it out.

It was her first day and all she'd done so far was eat three cheese Danishes. Amara needed to find her something to do before she picked up another one.

"How about you go home and get your laptop? That way we can start making a list of things we can do to get some business in here."

Daisy nodded and pulled her purse from underneath the cash register cabinet. "I'm telling you, Amara. The key to everything is going to be getting the students from the college in here."

"Well, that will be first on our list then. Go on, get."

Her cousin waved and walked out the front door. With Daisy gone, though, she no longer had anything to keep her mind off of Eric and how sexy he sounded when he groaned in her ear. That memory alone left her feeling like a tangled ball of nervous energy, ready to burst free.

She needed a distraction, and fast.

Amara looked around the bakery. She'd already cleaned out the refrigerator and refilled her spice rack earlier. The counter had already been wiped down more times than she could count. The floor shined—well, as much as it could, considering its condition.

She looked at the tray of doughnuts inside the bakery's smaller glass cabinet and was debating on whether to color-code them by frosting and cake color when her pregnant sister-in-law walked through the front door.

Thank God.

"The baby wants *polvorones*," Trina announced. "And he wants at least six. Don't judge."

Amara hugged her and they exchanged kisses on the cheek. "Who am I to judge you?" she told Trina. "I can eat four of those in one sitting and I'm not even pregnant!"

They both laughed, and she relaxed for the first time since Eric had walked out of the bakery. She fingered the letter securely nestled inside her jeans' front pocket. She'd brought it with her while she debated what do with it, but Trina's unexpected visit made the decision for her.

Amara set out two napkins on the bakery's single Formica-top table. Trina sat in one of the white plastic patio chairs, while Amara gave them each three of the disc-shaped cookies dusted in powdered sugar. As she pulled two water bottles from the refrigerated case near the cash register, she decided that her sister-in-law could tell her whether Miguel would want to know about Eric being back in town.

Time to open Pandora's box.

She let her finish one cookie before bringing up the subject. A hungry Trina was a distracted Trina and Amara needed her full attention for this very important conversation.

"So, you'll never guess who came into the bakery yesterday." She took a bite of her cookie and waited.

"Who?" asked Trina, after popping another cookie into her mouth.

"Eric Valencia." Amara tried to keep her voice nonchalant. But even saying his name quickened her pulse unexpectedly.

"Shut up!" Crumbs flew out of Trina's mouth and all over the small table. Eyes wide, she grabbed the bottle of water and gulped. "No way. No freaking way!"

Amara nodded.

"Is he back for good, or just visiting? Did he say where he's been for the last twelve years?"

"He didn't say. We, um, we didn't get a chance to talk that much actually."

Trina took another gulp of water. Her eyes narrowed. "Did he ask about Miguel?"

The concern in her voice tugged at Amara's heart. Of course Trina wanted to protect her husband. She'd been there on the day that Eric had skipped their graduation ceremony and left town without a word. The three of them — Miguel, Trina, and Eric — had all been part of the same group of friends. And after Eric left, Trina had come over to the house almost every day that summer to take Miguel out and keep him busy so he wouldn't miss the best friend who had deserted him. That's when the two of them had become a couple. So in a way, Eric helped push them together.

That is, after he'd ripped everything apart.

Amara pulled the envelope out of her pocket and slid it across the table in front of Trina. "He left this letter for Miguel."

Both of them looked at the envelope. "Did you read it?" Trina asked.

"No. I wanted to, but that wouldn't be right…right?"

"Right." She agreed. They continued staring at the envelope as if it might suddenly jump up and bite them. Given they had no idea what the letter said, it still just might.

"So what do you think? Do you want to give it to Miguel?" Amara held her breath.

Trina put her hand over her mouth and looked out the window. "I don't know what this will do to him…"

Amara knew what she meant. Miguel had thought of Eric like a brother. Although he never said it directly to her, she knew he missed his friend. Plus, a lot of people believed Miguel knew where Eric had gone all along.

But he didn't know. And after a few months, Miguel told everyone that he didn't care.

Trina put her hand on her stomach. "He should know. He deserves to know." She took the letter and stuck it inside her purse. They sat there in silence for a few minutes. Finally Trina pushed her napkin toward Amara. "Bartender, hit me again."

She nodded got up to fetch three more *polvorones*.

Trina closed her eyes and took a bite. "Seriously, these are the best things you've ever made."

Amara shrugged. "They're just shortbread cookies with chopped walnuts. All I'm doing is following my dad's recipe. I bet you could make them just as easy."

"No way. First of all, your brother married me for many reasons, but my baking skills were not one of them. Second of all, I've had your dad's *polvorones* and these are *way* better. They're just so buttery, sweet and…and…sinful."

An image of Eric's lips flashed before her eyes. Now

those were sinful.

"Hello? Amara?"

Trina's voice interrupted her impure thoughts about another part of Eric's body and the way it had grown hard and hot against her.

"I'm sorry, I was thinking about the recipe for the *polvorones*. I guess I did make a few small tweaks to it."

"See, I knew it. You need to give yourself more credit, honey. When are you going to start selling some of your own desserts here?"

Amara rolled her eyes. "Can we please not talk about that again? There was an unfortunate incident yesterday involving my mother and a *tres leches* cupcake that I'd rather not discuss."

Trina gave her a knowing smile. She'd had enough "incidents" of her own with Amara's mother to know not to push for further info. "Alrighty then. Let's talk about Eric. How did he look? Does he still have those killer eyelashes?"

The way Eric looked, or how he smelled, or how he kissed her was not something Amara wanted to discuss, either. She shot out of her chair and mumbled something about needing to clean up in case a customer walked in.

"Um, since I've been here, not one person has walked through those doors. Why are you acting all shifty-like?"

"I'm not acting shifty. Is that even a word? I just felt like getting up, you know, to let the cookies digest."

"What gives, my sister from another mister? Watcha freaking out about? Would it have anything to do with a certain dark-haired eyelash model from our past?"

Suddenly it seemed like a good time to start folding pastry boxes. What if a tour bus showed up with twenty customers wanting to buy a dozen cookies each? Better to be safe than sorry.

"Oh. My. God." Trina flew out of her chair and followed Amara around the bakery. "You *are* acting goofy because of Eric! Did he say something, did he do something?"

"No!"

Tiny hands grabbed her by both arms and turned her around. Trina's Cheshire cat grin told Amara she couldn't lie about what had happened between her and her brother's ex-best friend.

"Spill it, Amara Maria Robles. Or God help me, I'll will accidentally mention my suspicions in front of your mother!"

Trina had pulled out the big gun. Amara folded. "He kissed me," she muttered under breath and looked at her shoes.

"Huh? What did you say?"

Amara met Trina's eyes. "I said, 'He kissed me.'"

"Shut up!" Trina shoved Amara's right shoulder. "What a fucking pervert. I'm going to tell Miguel to kick his ass. We should have him arrested for attempted sexual assault."

Amara shook her head and waved her hands frantically. "No, you don't understand. I kissed him back!" Then she explained everything that had happened, from the minute he walked through the door to when he walked out.

Back at the table, Amara let out a long sigh and put her head in her hands. "I don't understand it. I haven't seen the guy in years and all of a sudden I want to jump his bones right there in the middle of my parents' kitchen!"

Her sister-in-law laughed like a hyena. "Okay, first of all honey, no one says 'jump his bones' anymore. You wanted to fuck him, plain and simple. Second of all, of course you wanted to fuck him. You've had a crush on him since you were thirteen or fourteen, right?"

Amara opened her eyes in shock. She didn't even know what to say.

"Sorry sister, but it was kind of obvious."

"You mean Eric knew that I…"

"Well, I did and I'm sure Miguel did. But, maybe not Eric. He was kind of oblivious about those kinds of things back then. Remember when that twit Mariah's car kept co-incidentally breaking down in front of your house on the days we were all there? I think it was only after the third of fourth time that Miguel finally slapped Eric on the back of the head and told him to ask her out."

The mention of Eric's girlfriend from high school twisted her gut into a giant knot.

Trina must've sensed it and reached out to pat Amara's hand. "So what are you going to do?"

"Well, I have to make the dough for tomorrow's batch of *polvorones*. You're probably going to wipe out my supply, right?"

"No, silly. Well, yes, I'm going to take everything you got. But no, that's not what I meant. I meant, what are you going to do about Eric?"

Should Amara confess that she'd been thinking about a possible second round of heavy kissing? Or more? Probably not. So she played dumb. "What do you mean? There's nothing to do, right?"

"Okay, I'm relieved to hear that. I don't even want to think of what your brother—or your parents—would do if you two got together."

"Why?"

"You know why."

"I know that he's made some mistakes, but that was a long time ago. He seems like he's different, like he wants to make things right. Maybe that's what the letter to Miguel is all about?"

She shrugged. "I don't know. I guess it will be up to your brother to decide. Either way, he's not really your type, right?"

"Don't. Just don't. My mother basically said the same exact thing."

"Well, you know I always have your back when it comes to Consuelo, but I have to admit that in this case she's right. Eric was my friend, too, but even I knew he had issues. Just because he's older doesn't mean those issues have gone away. Getting involved with him will only cause lots of unnecessary drama. You don't need that in your life, honey."

"Oh my gosh. I'm so tired of people telling me what I need and don't need in my life. I'm not a little kid!" Amara pushed herself away from the table and walked into the kitchen. She knew Trina would follow her. And after a few seconds she did.

"Whoa there," her sister-in-law said from the doorway. "What's with all the yelling? I'm just offering an opinion. I'm not telling you what to do."

"Funny. That's what my mom always says. You know, after she tells me what to do."

"Wait," Trina said. "First I agree with Consuelo, and now I'm talking like her? I think I need to sit down."

They laughed and Amara gave Trina a hug. "I'm sorry I yelled at you. You didn't deserve that."

"It's okay. And you're right. It's no one else's business who you want to date or sleep with. I promise to keep my big pregnant butt out of your love life from now on."

"Amara has a love life! With who?"

Both of them turned and saw Daisy standing in the doorway.

"Nobody." Amara sighed and hoped against hope her cousin wouldn't ask any more questions. Luckily, the jingle of the front door interrupted any more grilling. "Daisy, can you go help that customer, please?"

"Fine, don't tell me," she muttered and stomped back out.

Trina rolled her eyes and laughed. "I still can't believe she's working here."

"Well, working isn't exactly the word I'd use. She's supposed to be helping me with some marketing stuff for the bakery but all she's done so far is gobble up half of my inventory. She may be tiny, but that girl can eat."

"God, I'd kill for her metabolism. And her perky boobs. I'm going to need them after breastfeeding this little guy," Trina said, pointing to her rounded belly.

"Thank you for saying that stuff earlier about not meddling in my love life. Even if it was just part of a master plan to get more cookies."

"You see right through me, don't you?"

Amara chuckled and hugged her sister-in-law again. "I'll grab some for you to take home."

"Hey, why don't you come over tomorrow and make me food?" Trina asked while Amara packed her a box of cookies. "Just kidding. We'll order pizza for dinner and watch rich housewives scream at each other and knock over tables."

"Sorry, but I can't. Daisy and I are making a cake for the Lozanos' baby's baptism in the morning and then I have to deliver it to the party at 5 p.m."

"So deliver it and then come over. Bring Daisy, too.

Housewives are known to be fashionably late."

Amara handed her the box. "Well, Daisy might be able to go, but I have to stay after I deliver the cake because my parents can't. They have that concert tomorrow at the Hollywood Bowl. So I need to represent and make sure that everyone at the party knows that the cake is from the Robles Panaderia."

Trina agreed to a rain check for the following weekend, and promised Amara she'd give Miguel the letter after he got home from work.

Later, as she rolled the dough for another batch of cookies, she thought about Trina's reaction to her kiss with Eric. She'd automatically assumed he'd done something wrong. Maybe she should've given the letter directly to her brother instead? That way she could tell him herself that he seemed different and encourage Miguel to give him a chance.

Then maybe Eric would be coming around more often.

Well, who says you can't go to him?

The nagging little voice of reason inside her head, that's who. She'd never pursued a man in her life, especially not one with a devilish grin and reputation to match. She'd never done a lot of things and it occurred to her that might be her problem. No wonder she hadn't had sex in almost a year. If she continued listening to what others thought she needed, she'd never get what she really wanted. And right now, that was Eric.

Amara ignored the nagging voice and decided that if she didn't hear from him by Monday, she'd go pay him a visit and offer to reach out to her brother on his behalf.

At least, that's what she planned on telling anyone if they ever found out.

Chapter Four

The looks and whispers began as soon as he arrived at the party to pick up his *abuela*. He knew what they were saying even if he didn't hear every word.

He's probably a drunk now like his dad. How long before he ends up in jail? How many women has he knocked up since high school?

The whispers didn't hurt him, only irritated him, and he tried to shake them off as he searched for his *abuela*. He finally found her in the kitchen sitting with a group of women.

"*Mijo*! What are you doing here?"

"It's already seven. Mom sent me to come take you home." From the corner of his eye, he saw ice-cold glares being thrown in his direction.

"I told her to come for me at seven-thirty. She was supposed to get me on her way home from work."

"She's going to go to dinner with some friends so she told me to come instead."

"But they haven't even cut the cake yet," she explained and pointed to a massive sheet cake decorated with white frosting and eerily realistic blue and yellow sugar roses. "The Robles girl brought it only a few minutes ago."

A rugged breath escaped his lungs as all the blood in his body rushed south. It had only been a day since he'd seen or touched Amara, and that had been one fucking day too long. He was already going through withdrawals. Forgetting about her had proved harder than he'd originally thought. Perhaps if he just talked to her for a few minutes, even tried to be her friend again, then maybe he'd remember that she was too nice to ever be the naughty minx he'd dreamt about after those searing kisses.

"Okay, we can stay until they cut the cake," he told his grandmother. "I'll just go wait for you outside." She nodded and shooed him away, oblivious to the looks of death coming from the silver-haired mob in the corner.

He walked through the open sliding glass door and stepped onto the house's backyard patio. Blue and white streamers hung from the awning, and blue balloons dotted each wooden pillar. Tables filled with food lined the brick wall, and his stomach grumbled. But Eric wasn't hungry for food.

As he made his way through the zigzag of tables and folding chairs, he looked around for his target. Music blared into the evening air. Chairs scraped against the concrete as guests stood up and gathered in the middle of the large patio and began dancing. Strobe lights lit up two opposite corners of the backyard and the crowd cheered. He doubted if the guest of honor—the newborn baby boy who had just been baptized—realized that his party would go on well after his bedtime.

The glare of one strobe light illuminated a corner of the detached garage and that's when Eric spotted her. She stood against the wall, sipping a drink, and looking beyond bored.

He approached her just as the song stopped. "Hey."

She gasped, nearly upending her drink. "Eric! I didn't... um...what are you doing here?"

"Catching you by surprise, judging by the look on your face." He winked and then smiled as he surveyed the rest of her. Her dark, wild curls flowed onto her perfect breasts, which barely peeked over the neckline of a blue sleeveless blouse. Her curvy hips and ample ass were accentuated by a simple black skirt that stopped just above her knees.

And just like that, he grew hard, thinking about what she was wearing underneath that skirt. To make matters worse, the way she peered up at him through her thick eyelashes— while licking her lips, damn it—made it nearly impossible *not* to think of what she could do with that tongue. If he were a praying man, he'd get down on his knees and ask God to give him the strength to walk away then and just go home.

But he had nothing to go home to.

And Amara was right there, in her tight, little skirt and nearly sheer blouse, looking at him as if she were offering every dirty fantasy he could think of.

There were a lot of them.

If he kept this up, his dick would punch through his pants. Desperate, he tried for small talk. "The cake looks nice," he said, leaning in so she could hear him over the music. "You did a good job."

"Thanks!" The bright smile she gave him nearly sent him to his knees. "I had some problems with the frosting. It took a lot longer to set than usual. I was supposed to drop it off two hours ago."

"I'm sure it tastes amazing," he said.

Just like *her.*

She said something back to him but he couldn't hear because of the ridiculously loud, thumping music. If they were going to have a real conversation, he needed to get closer. Not the brightest idea he ever had, especially since he already had to lean in every time he spoke, but he didn't see a way around it. Nor did he want to.

He moved closer, his head next to hers, his lips hovering barely an inch away from her ear. How easy it would be to nip her earlobe and soothe it with his tongue. "What are you drinking?" he asked.

He allowed himself to trail the tip of his nose along her neck and inhaled a whiff of vanilla mixed with other fragrant spices. Fuck, she even *smelled* appetizing. And that triggered a hunger to taste her again—but this time he wouldn't stop at her mouth. His groin tightened further at the image of Amara on her back, her legs spread open, waiting for him to taste her there. A groan escaped him and without thinking, he took another step closer.

She looked up at him, her cheeks flushed and her chest heaving with deep breaths. "I don't know what it is, actually. Someone just shoved it in my hand. I'm not really a drinker."

He lifted her hair from her neck and swept it behind her back. "Me, either." At least not anymore, he thought.

She reached for his hand. "How are your fingers?"

"Better," he said, watching her turn it over in her hand. "Must have been your first aid skills."

Her light laugh danced between them, making him

focus on her luscious lips. They were pink and glistening with whatever concoction was inside that red cup. The urge to lick the drops away barreled over any remaining resolve to keep things platonic between them tonight.

And she still hadn't let go of his hand.

Fuck willpower, he decided. He hadn't given up drinking overnight. What made him think giving up his attraction to Amara would be any different?

He closed the few remaining inches between them, pinning her between his body and the wall. She gasped, but when she didn't object, he pressed his body against hers.

"What are you doing?" she breathed.

He let his lips brush her earlobe and nipped it, just once, before laying all of his cards on the table. "I'm showing you that I haven't stopped thinking about you. And I don't know what the fuck it was I ever did to deserve the privilege to kiss the hell out of those lips, but I'd sacrifice just about anything right now if it meant I could do it again."

Even in the shadows, he could see her eyes widen. She turned to face him. "You would? I thought you wouldn't want to after realizing who I was."

He couldn't help smiling at the fact she'd nailed his response exactly. "I admit I was a little shocked. Okay, a lot shocked. And truth is, me and you probably isn't the best idea I've ever had. But I've never been shy about telling people what I want. And, sweetheart, I want you so bad I can't walk straight."

The colors of the strobe light danced across her face and his gaze traveled to her mouth. When she licked her bottom lip again, the heat between them intensified by a million degrees. Time to see if there was a minx inside her after all.

He pressed in tight so there'd be no misunderstanding about what he was about to say. "In fact, there's nothing more in this world that I want right now than to push you up against this wall and fuck you. But there are too many people around and someone could see us."

She watched the crowd for a few seconds before meeting his eyes again. Had he scared her off? Would she pull her hand away and tell him he'd misinterpreted everything? He waited for her to bring him back to harsh reality. Instead, she opened her mouth and changed everything.

"Then let's go somewhere so they can't."

· · ·

Maybe it was the wanton beat of the thumping music or the ounce of alcohol in her system. Either way, she'd just told Eric that she wanted to be alone with him. And although she didn't use the exact words, she was pretty sure she'd just agreed to have sex with him, too.

She followed him through the crowd, not knowing where they were going. Did people notice that they were holding hands? It didn't seem like it. Everyone was too busy dancing and having a good time. Bodies bumped into her and stepped on her feet, but she didn't care. She just walked faster. Bumped back harder. Gripped Eric's hand tighter.

Amara couldn't believe this wasn't just one of those dreams that felt real but disappeared the moment you opened your eyes. Only yesterday she'd been fantasizing about what would happen the next time they saw each other. After being reminded, yet again, by Trina that she should stay away, she'd been more determined than ever to do the opposite. Thoughts of what they'd do together had consumed her for the rest of the day. So much so that she'd found herself in the shower after 11 p.m., seeking much-needed release via a strategically placed showerhead.

But in the morning light, old insecurities needled at her. Sure, he'd wanted to kiss her when he thought she was just some random big-busted girl who worked in his former friend's bakery. But the shocking realization of who she really was—not to mention her mother's little scene—most likely doused any budding attraction to her.

What if she had followed through on her initial plan to seduce him and then he rejected her? She'd die. Absolutely die. It had been a foolish idea to think she could handle being with a guy like Eric. She was more the speed of a merry-go-round at an amusement park, whereas he was the lightning fast rollercoaster. Her libido had been bigger than her courage, so she'd pushed the silly idea out of her head that morning as she worked on the cake for the party.

So when Eric walked up to her, she'd told herself it would be better to pretend that she hadn't given a second thought to what had happened between them. She'd told herself to be polite, chat for a few minutes and say good-bye for good. But the closer he moved to her, the harder it had been to walk away. Asking to see his burns had only been an excuse to touch him. Then he'd touched *her*. Her hair, her neck, her earlobe…God, the earlobe…rekindling the need to kiss him, too.

And then he said he wanted her.

All her life, Amara had done what other people thought she should do rather than follow her own desires. It was time to do what *she* wanted to do. What she'd ached to do ever since she saw Eric walk into the bakery.

And now she had her chance.

You are going to have sex with Eric Valencia. He is going to have sex with you. Don't you dare ruin this by overthinking everything. You are a grown woman who can have sex when she wants and with whom she wants without it meaning anything.

Because it couldn't.

He led her around the guesthouse next to the large swimming pool, but swore when they came upon small circles of people smoking and drinking behind it. They turned back around and continued down a concrete pathway, the music behind them but still pulsating through her. He stopped and pointed. She followed his finger toward the pathway as it curved down a grassy incline and ended at a small shed-like building.

"There. We can go in there."

Amara's heart quickened as they raced down the hill. They were both out of the breath when they landed at the building's small, elevated porch. Eric tried the door but it was locked. "Damn it!" He looked around and turned his attention to a cluster of clay pots and figurines grouped near the doorway. One by one he picked them up, turning them over in search of something, but never once letting go of her hand.

"No one ever really locks the gardener's shed. There has to be a spare key here somewhere." He turned over the one that looked like an evil squirrel and a silver key attached to a thick cord tumbled out.

"Yes!" He grabbed it off the ground and inserted it into the lock. With one click, the door opened.

Eric pulled her inside and used her to push the door closed. He crushed his body against hers, seizing her mouth in a frenzied, hard kiss that took her breath away. She kissed him back, opening her mouth to find his tongue. He ran his hands up the back of her thighs and under her skirt, settling on each butt cheek. With every squeeze, he thrust his groin against her belly.

"Tell me what you want," he growled. "I want to hear you say it."

Her voice caught in her throat. Whenever she tried to speak, only breathless sighs came out.

"Do you want me touch you?" He moved his lips to her neck and collarbone.

She could only nod. He groaned and worked at the buttons on her blouse, eventually tearing it open with both of his hands. The cool night air slammed against her exposed skin but she didn't shiver. Eric's hands left a trail of heat in their wake. He pulled her bra down and consumed one full breast after the other. Amara quivered, her climax building with every touch.

When he flicked his tongue against one straining nipple, she couldn't contain herself any longer.

"I...oh...don't..," she gasped, grabbing his hair with her fingers. She teetered on the edge. Only one more thing would surely cause her to fall. But she couldn't bring herself say it.

"You're going to come, aren't you?" His breath burned hot and heavy against her bare skin. But she could only whimper a response. Despite her lack of words, he got the message. He moved one hand from her bottom to yank down her panties. "Fuuuck, you're so wet," he groaned as his fingers slid between her folds.

His touch, combined with his crude words, obliterated any sense of self-control. She dug her nails into his shoulders and let go.

Eric captured her scream with his mouth as the orgasm ripped through her. She saw stars and swirls of red and orange. Her knees gave way, but he held her up with strong, protective hands and buried his face in the crook of her neck. When the quaking finally subsided, he kissed her nose and reached down to pull up her underwear.

Although her lust had been satiated for the moment, her pulsing core still yearned for deeper fulfillment. Why wasn't Eric dropping his pants?

"What are you doing?" she asked as he started to redo the buttons on her blouse. "I thought you wanted to…you know…"

He grinned as he moved a wisp of hair from her eyes. "I did. I do. But not like this."

"Did I do something wrong? I don't understand."

Eric grabbed her face with both of his hands and gently kissed her. "You didn't do anything wrong. But let's face it, you're not exactly the kind of girl who has sex in a dirty shed during a baby's baptism party."

She knew he meant it as a compliment, but that didn't stop her stomach from turning. Her mother always complained that Amara liked to push people to say things they didn't want to say. Usually, she ended up regretting pushing so hard. But she couldn't help it. Just like now.

She moved away from Eric. Then she asked the question she already knew she didn't want the answer to. "So what kind of girl am I, exactly?"

"Huh? What are you talking about?"

"You said I'm not the kind of girl who has sex in a shed. So I want to know what kind of girl you think I am."

"You know."

"Maybe I don't. Tell me."

"Why are you doing this?"

"Tell me."

"Amara…"

"Eric, just say it. I want to hear you say it."

"Fine! You're a nice girl, Amara, and I'm trying really hard to be a nice guy."

She pulled away from him and straightened her skirt. "So let me get this straight. *You've* decided that this isn't the right time or place for *me* to have sex."

"Well, not just you. I thought it would be better if our first time was somewhere, you know, less dirty." He frowned. "I want it to be, I don't know, *nice* I guess."

There was that word again. She clenched her hands into fists and struggled to not scream. She was so tired of people associating that word with her. She didn't want "nice" sex. She'd had enough of nice sex with her old college boyfriend, "Mr. Missionary." For once in her life, she wanted splinters-in-your-back-hair-pulling-lip-biting-crazy-hard-hot-sex.

And it crushed her that Eric had decided she couldn't have it—at least not with him. She was really getting sick of people who felt they knew what was best for her without asking her what *she* wanted.

He touched her shoulder but she flinched as if he had slapped her. He opened his mouth, thought better of it, and closed it again.

But when Amara reached for the door, he finally exploded. "I'm not going to fuck you in a fucking shed, okay?

Why is that such a big deal? You still had a good time, right? Or was that someone else coming all over my hand?"

That was it. Amara had officially hit her mortification limit. "You're right, Eric, I did have a good time. Thank you very much for my orgasm. Good night."

She threw open the door. She kicked her way through the jungle of clay pots on the ground, not caring if they broke or ruined her shoes. Tears threatened to fall, but she rubbed them away before they left the rim of her eye. He yelled her name behind her, each time sounding a little bit closer. She just walked faster and faster up the hill until a hand grabbed her wrist and stopped her in her tracks.

He'd done nothing wrong really, yet she could barely stand to look at him.

"What the hell is wrong with you?" His forehead glistened in the glare of the full moon and his breath came in gasps. "Why are trying to push me away now? I thought you wanted this."

She *had* wanted it. She *still* wanted it. And she was both angry and embarrassed that Eric had decided she couldn't have it. At least not tonight. Since when had he become so chivalrous?

Despite her desire, Amara reined in her emotions and tried to salvage some shreds of her evaporating dignity.

"I'm sorry. You were right. I'm not the kind of girl who has sex in sheds. I should have never let things get so out of hand." He reached for her but she shook her head and took a step back. "I can't be with someone like you. I thought I wanted to be, but I was wrong."

She turned to walk away when he grabbed her wrist again. With one swift pull, her body slammed against his. He still held her wrist with one hand, while the other gripped her rounded bottom.

His mouth came down to only inches from hers. Her eyes widened as she felt a hardness grow behind the zipper of his jeans. Trembling knees caused her to lose her balance, so he held her tighter. Any resistance or guilt started to slip away. She licked her lips in anticipation.

But he didn't kiss her. Instead, he stared into her eyes and whispered, "Oh, I get it. The good girl is going to pretend now that she wasn't about to get down and dirty with the bad boy. If it helps you sleep tonight, then go right ahead and act like you don't want my cock inside you right this very minute. But do you want to know what's going to help me sleep tonight, sweetheart? Remembering the look in your eyes when I made you come. So pretend all you want and then when you're ready to stop playing these silly games and start acting like a woman who needs to be fucked long, hard, and often, I'll be happy to give you what you need."

This time it was Eric who walked away. And Amara let him.

Chapter Five

Eric walked into the Pasadena sports bar with only one thought on his mind.

If Miguel knocked him out, how in the hell would he get home?

He probably should've figured that out beforehand. Oh well. Nothing he could do about it now. Eric surveyed the room and noticed only a handful of people sat in booths or at the counter—not the crowd the bar probably got on a Friday or Saturday night. And since there were no major games on this particular Tuesday evening, he had his pick of seats.

A sports bar wasn't exactly the best place for a recovering alcoholic, but Miguel had suggested it and Eric wasn't in a position to make any demands as to where their first meeting should take place. At least it wasn't a deserted alley.

That meant there would be some witnesses in case his ex-best friend decided to throw a punch at him as a form of payback. Eric decided he'd let him get in one good shot. He owed that to him at least.

As he looked around the room for an empty table, he saw Miguel already sitting in a corner booth, studying a bottle of beer. His ex-friend looked up just as Eric approached the table, and gave him a curt nod of acknowledgment. Eric nodded back.

It was their customary greeting, even when they were in junior high school. Of course, neither of them looked very much like they did back then. Miguel appeared to have finally grown into his six-foot frame. He was still thin, but far from the gangly teenager he had been. His old buzz cut was gone, replaced by a short, spikey style. He wore a dark blue business suit, complete with jacket and tie. Eric wished he'd worn a polo shirt with his jeans rather than a black Lakers T-shirt. Their choice of outfits made the difference between the old friends even more obvious.

"Hey man," he said as he took his seat across the table.

"Hey." Miguel took a drink of his beer and signaled to the waitress standing by the bar. "You want a beer?"

He did. Desperately. But he didn't trust himself.

The waitress arrived at their table and waited for his order. "Uh, I'll just take a Coke or Pepsi, whatever you got." He glanced at Miguel, who raised his eyebrow and then ordered himself another beer.

"Eric Valencia turning down a beer? I can't believe it," Miguel said after the waitress left.

"Well, believe it. Me and alcohol aren't really friends anymore." He shouldn't have put it like that, he realized, the second after he said it.

Miguel shifted in his seat. "So how long has it been since you quit?"

"Let's see." He did some quick math in his head. "It's been 536 days."

"Good for you, man. I don't think I could give this up cold turkey." Miguel pointed to the empty bottle in front of him.

Eric laughed, "Well you probably don't have a problem with it like I did."

"You know, you were the one who gave me my first beer."

"I remember. I also gave you your second, third, and fourth. I had to drag your drunk ass home two blocks that night."

"Yeah. Didn't I puke on your shoes or something?"

"No. You puked on yours."

They laughed, and for the first time since coming back, Eric felt like he'd never left.

His old friend stared out the window as the waitress returned with their drinks. He figured it was time to rip off the Band-Aid. "I shouldn't have disappeared the way I did. I shouldn't have ditched you like that," Eric said when she left. "I shouldn't have done a lot of things. I just wanted to tell you that, you know, face to face."

Miguel nodded. "So tell me. Where've you been for the past twelve years?"

"Las Vegas, aka Sin City. Seems fitting, doesn't it?"

Eric could laugh now. But there was nothing funny about his life after he left L.A. "When I turned twenty-one, that's when the drinking really got out of hand. I realized I could stay all day in a casino playing the penny slots and get all the free beer I wanted. I tried to quit but by then I had gotten into construction. Headed up my own company. It was good money that bought me even more beer. Then I started showing up late or calling off sick."

"What made you finally quit?"

"A friend. With his help, I got cleaned up and straightened out. And life for a while wasn't that bad. Then the economy tanked, people stopped buying homes in Vegas, and that was the end of my business."

"Wow. That's rough, man." Miguel looked like he actually felt bad for him. "Did you keep in touch with your family at least?"

"Not at first. I assumed everyone from my past had moved on and forgotten about me."

"We did move on. After so many months, most of us figured you were either in jail or dead."

"Sometimes I'm surprised I'm not."

The realization hung heavily between them. Miguel cleared his throat and took another swig of his beer before asking the million-dollar question, "So what made you come back, then?"

"My *abuela* had a heart attack. I came back to take care of her during the day while my mom is at work, and I'm looking for temp jobs that I can do at night so eventually I can get my business going again. I guess you can say I came back to start over."

After a few seconds of uncomfortable silence, he spoke again. "Since you had your own company, I'm assuming that means you know how to put up drywall and paint?"

"Yeah. I can do that, plus lay tile and other kinds of flooring." He laughed and took another sip of his soda. "Why? You need some carpet installed?"

"Actually, not carpet, but laminate flooring. And some other handyman kind of tasks. I'm supposed to be helping my dad fix up the bakery, but I just don't have time. Plus with the baby coming, I could use some extra hands—if you're interested."

"Definitely. But I doubt your mom would let me help out. I got the feeling she didn't want me around your...you."

"She's going to have a fit, no doubt about that, but I can talk her into it. I'm giving that woman her first grandchild— she'll do just about anything for me right now."

They both laughed and the tension in his neck and shoulders eased off. Miguel told him about a few more items that needed to be done. Eric assured him that he could do it all.

"And I'm sure my dad won't mind if you do the work after the bakery closes," Miguel continued. "It's not that busy during the day, but it sounds like working at night would be better for you anyway. Plus, you won't have to worry about Amara."

Eric coughed and sputtered as soda went down his windpipe. "What do you mean?"

"You know, her getting in your way and stuff. Remember how much she used to bug us when we'd hang out at my house? She can still be annoying like that."

He wiped his mouth and shrugged. "She seemed fine when I ran into her at the bakery."

"Yeah, she's fine in small doses. Don't get me wrong. I love my little sister, but I pity the next guy she dates. He's going to be in for it."

Eric played with the straw in his glass and tried to keep his voice even as he asked, "So, she's not dating anyone right now?"

"Nope. Well, not that I know of. She's...wait a minute,"

Miguel said, his eyes narrowing. "Why do you want to know, Valencia?"

"No reason. I…I was just curious, that's all."

Miguel leaned forward, with his forearms pressed on the table. "Listen, just because we're cool now, doesn't mean everything is the same as before," he said, his voice hard and stern. "I'm okay with you doing the remodel but I'm not okay with you going anywhere near my sister."

"So what am I supposed to do? Pretend she doesn't exist? Isn't she at the bakery all the time?"

"You can talk to her if you happen to run into her, that's fine. But things will be much better for everyone—especially you—if you keep your hands to yourself, get it? This is serious, man. I need you to promise me that you won't try anything with Amara."

If it had been anyone else asking, Eric would've laughed in his face. But he owed Miguel, especially now, when he was offering him a job. He figured it was a reasonable request, and the motivation he needed to stick to his plan to stay the hell away from her. Sure, he'd meant everything he'd said the other night, about being willing to fuck her when she was ready. That didn't mean he'd die if he didn't. He'd been attracted to women before and eventually that attraction wore off. It was bound to happen with Amara, too. So sacrificing one night between her legs was worth it if it meant he'd be one job closer to fixing his sorry life.

"I promise I won't try anything with your sister," he told Miguel.

Then he tapped his glass against his former friend's beer to seal the deal.

Chapter Six

Thirteen, fourteen, fifteen, sixteen, seventeen, thirteen, fourteen.

Wait. What?

Amara looked at the tray of eggs and tried to remember where her counting had gone wrong. Realizing the eggs weren't going to tell her anything, she scratched out the pencil marks on her notepad and sighed. She despised taking inventory, but she needed something to keep her busy and keep her mind off the fact that Eric was in the front of the bakery talking measurements and paint colors with her dad. They'd been there only about half an hour, and in that time, she'd counted lemons (five), bags of walnuts (two), cans of coconut milk (nine) and now the eggs. Well, not really the eggs, because every time she'd get to sixteen or seventeen, she'd lose her concentration.

She'd been out of sorts all week and hadn't been able to focus on much of anything except what Eric had said and done to her on the night of the party. At first, she was still pretty embarrassed and angry. Once those emotions simmered down, though, naughty rebellious ones rose back up. Especially when she found out that Miguel had met with Eric, and then had somehow convinced their dad to hire him.

Over the past few days, in between frosting cakes and rolling out *tortillas*, she'd thought of ways to approach Eric and casually mention that she was ready, willing, and able to have sex with him. But all those ideas went out the window as soon as he walked into the bakery that morning with her dad. He'd barely acknowledged her presence, let alone shown her that he was still interested in her that way.

Ugh. Men could be so frustrating some times.

She shook off the frustration and stared earnestly at the purple cardboard tray filled with eggs.

One, two, three, four, five, six, seven…

"We don't need to do too much in here. Some drawers need fixing and maybe you can put in a new ceiling fan, but nothing else. *Es todo.* No one is going to be coming in here except Amara. And she doesn't care how the kitchen looks, right *mija*?"

Apparently it was a rhetorical question because, after chuckling to himself, her dad showed Eric which drawers needed repairing. Good thing he hadn't expected her to answer. Her pencil and her ability to talk froze as soon as she heard them walk in. She continued looking at the eggs, but in the corner of her eye she could make out Eric's worn blue jeans and black work boots.

One, two, three, four, five, six…

"Okay, that should be it. You stay here while I run across the street to the house to get my wallet. Then we can go in your truck to Home Depot to buy the supplies."

Her head shot up just in time to see her dad heading back toward the front of the bakery.

"Sure. I'll wait here for you," she heard Eric say. "I think I'm going to buy one of those banana muffins. I didn't eat breakfast this morning."

Her dad waved him off. "Amara, go get Eric whatever he wants. He's giving me a good deal for this job, so his money is no good here, *entiendes*?"

She nodded and followed her dad out of the kitchen. The tiny hairs on the back of her neck signaled that Eric followed behind her. Willing herself not to shake like a wet dog, she carefully took the plastic tongs hanging on the side of the counter and retrieved a muffin from the top display rack. He had moved to the other side of the counter to face her. She cleared her throat.

Play it cool, Amara. If he wasn't going to bring up the other night then she wouldn't either.

"Do you want it in a bag or on a plate?" she asked, hating the slight tremble in her voice.

"In a bag is fine. I'm going to eat it while I'm driving your dad to the store."

She met his eyes and she thought she saw something flash behind them. Probably just hunger, she thought, as she dropped the muffin into a small white bag. She didn't hand it to him, though. She didn't want to risk any contact, so she placed it on top of the counter. "There you go. Enjoy."

As she made a move to leave, he stopped her by calling out her name.

"I think we need to talk," he said.

Stuffing her hands into the side pockets of her beige cargo pants, Amara moved closer to the edge of the counter.

"I don't have anything to say."

He shrugged back. "Fine. But I do. What happened at the baptism party was—"

Amazing. Hot. Something she'd like to do again.

His stiffened posture and solemn expression hinted those weren't the same words he was going to use. It was what she had feared. He'd changed his mind. So she wanted him to think that she had to.

"That night was a mistake," she blurted before he could continue. She waited for him to argue back.

"Yes, it was," he said instead. His eyes didn't betray a bit of emotion. Neither did his tone. "I've done things I'm not proud of and I'm trying really hard to make up for those things by being a decent guy. And decent guys don't act the way I've been acting around you, so I'm going to stop. Especially now that Miguel's convinced your parents to give me this job. I can't risk messing this up. And I think that if something were to happen between us, well, that would be a distraction we both don't need right now."

Her legs wobbled. She moved her hands out of her pockets and gripped the counter to steady herself.

When she didn't answer back, he continued. "Anyway, I just wanted to make it clear that while I'm working here you don't have to worry about me doing anything…inappropriate. I probably won't even see you that much since I'm doing most of the work at night, but when I do, I promise to keep my hands and, um, other body parts to myself." He coughed out the last words and then shifted his weight from one foot to the other.

She'd been telling herself not to look directly at his mouth as he talked, so of course that's all she did. Even now, she couldn't stop.

So they stood there staring at each other. No words. No noise. She heard only the *tick, tick* of the bakery's wall clock and her own heart pounding in her ears. Then, heavy breaths. First hers, then his.

The A/C clicked on. A fan whirred in the background. Someone's breathing deepened. Probably hers, as she continued staring at his lips—not too thin, not too full—just perfect. Perfect for kissing. And sucking. Her mind flooded with images of those lips on hers—and not the ones on her mouth. It was her turn to shift her legs.

"God damn it, Amara," he groaned, almost as if he could see the images inside her head. "We need to forget what happened that night and move on. It's the right thing to do."

The gruffness of his voice surprised her. So did her own increasing disappointment. Unlike the night of the baptism party, she decided to hold it together and let him think she didn't care either way.

"Maybe you're right," she said.

"I *am* right." He shoved his hands into his pockets and stared at the floor. "Trust me, Amara. I'm a bastard. My life is fucked up. And as much as I would love to know how it feels to plunge my cock between your thighs, it's better for both of us if I never find out."

He turned and stalked out the front door, leaving Amara staring after him with her jaw on the floor.

Heat radiated from her chest and neck, so she dashed over to the refrigerated case and stuck her head as far in as she could get. Maybe she'd cool off before someone walked in.

I would love to know how it feels to plunge my cock

between your thighs.

She'd need another hour in the cooler, at least.

After a good ten minutes spent inventing every cupcake concoction she could think of—including a few flavors she wouldn't dare sell in a store, but sounded great for, say, licking off of Eric's abs—she felt cool enough to take a step backward, shut the door, and go back to the counter. That's when she noticed the bag with the muffin still sitting there—a reminder that there'd be no escaping Eric. He was back in her life for good.

Well, at least for the next few weeks.

She'd have to figure out a way to handle being around him. Because even though he was the one trying to do the convincing this time, she knew by the way he looked at her that he still wanted her. And that knowledge alone made heat pool between her thighs.

She ran back to the refrigerated case and stuck her head inside one more time.

• • •

Amara watched Daisy nibble on the last of the *buñuelos* she'd made that morning and had put out on a plate for customers to sample. Now, only small, shattered pieces remained of the fried *tortillas* sprinkled with cinnamon and sugar.

"Since we don't have any customers, why don't we brainstorm some more marketing ideas?"

She'd overheard her parents the previous night, talking about being short for this month's loan payment. If they couldn't pay back the loan on time, the bank would foreclose on their house. Her parents would be forced to live in the small apartment above their nice, newly remodeled bakery. It was filled with cobwebs and boxes and layers of dust, and Amara doubted if any people had ever lived there. Her mother had hyperventilated at the thought of being the first.

She'd left Chicago to save the bakery. It was time to get serious.

"*Fine*," Daisy groaned and dusted the cinnamon sugar from her hands. "How about we change the name of the bakery to something more…more sexy."

Amara rolled her eyes. "Okay, first of all, a bakery is not sexy. And second of all, my parents would never agree to change the name. Period. Try again."

"Excuse me, but a bakery can be sexy. Look around you. Whipped cream? Stuffed rolls? Hot buns? That's it! We can call it 'Robles' Hot Buns.'" She looked at Amara and they both burst out laughing.

"I don't care what you say," Daisy continued after they calmed down. "I think that would be a fabulous name for a bakery. And I think that guy Eric would be the perfect poster boy. Just think about it. We could stick his buns on fliers, billboards, on these napkins. What woman wouldn't want to put their lips on his fine ass?"

Her cousin had a valid point. But Amara wasn't going to give her any more ammunition. After Eric had come back that morning to retake some measurements, they'd done an awkward dance of "Let's not say too much or get too close." Daisy had grilled her as soon as he left. Amara denied that there was anything between them.

"The fact that you are neither confirming nor denying the hotness of his buns leads me to believe that I was right the first time—there is something going on," she pushed.

"I already told you—"

"Correction. You already lied to me. I know he's the guy you and Trina were talking about the other day."

Amara ignored her and walked into the kitchen to get more sugar packets. Daisy followed her.

"Okay fine. You won't tell me what really happened, so I'll have to let my wild imagination take a guess."

Amara grabbed a handful of packets from the box in the pantry and headed back to the front of the bakery with Daisy on her heels.

"Let's see. You guys hooked up after you saw him hammering something...hard. Nah. That's too boring," she said. "Did he take you on the kitchen counter? Ooh, or maybe right here against the display case?"

"We didn't have sex!"

"Ah, is there a 'yet' at the end of that sentence?"

"What? No. Of course not."

"Why not? He's hot, and judging by the way you stammered when he asked you where he could leave his tools for tonight, you are obviously into him. So what's the problem?"

"He's not my type."

"Puh-leeze woman. He's everyone's type! Try again."

"That's exactly what I mean. He can have any woman he wants. He probably does. And I don't do casual, uh, sex."

"Again I ask, why not? I don't care what battery operated toy you might have in your drawer, nothing beats the real thing. Even if it's only a one-time thing."

Amara couldn't hide her shock even if she tried. Her cousin was a year younger than she was and Amara had always thought of her more as a little sister—innocent and naive. Obviously, that wasn't the case anymore.

Daisy continued. "Besides, who said it would have to be casual? Maybe it could turn into something more? You'll never know if you don't at least try."

"No, it would never work. My parents…"

"He's not a serial killer, Amara. He's not a felon, right? What's the problem? And anyway, who cares what Ricardo and Consuelo think?"

"I know them. It would just turn into a big deal, and for what? It's not worth it."

"But how do you know for sure?" Daisy walked over and took the sugar packets out of her hand. Amara rolled her eyes, but her cousin didn't give up. "You know when you opened that little cupcake shop downtown? I was so proud of you. You were finally doing something for you, just you. But then…"

Amara cocked an eyebrow. "It crashed and burned and I lost all of my parents' money?"

Daisy pointed a handful of sugar packets at her. "Hey, that wasn't your fault. You were just ahead of your time. Look at all of the cupcake shops now. They're on every corner, just like freaking Starbucks."

"You know my mom wouldn't talk to me for a week after that? And it doesn't matter that I already paid them back. She still brings it up when she's really mad."

"The point is, you did it. And when it didn't work out, you picked yourself back up again and got that job in Chicago. But now it's like…"

"Like what?"

"Like you're settling for what your parents always wanted for you—to take over the bakery, get married to someone like your brother, and pop out a few grandkids," Daisy said, setting the sugar on the counter. "I'm just wondering when you're going to stop doing what everybody expects you to do and start doing the things *you* want to do?"

She bristled at her cousin's words, but only because Daisy was right.

It was time to shake things up around here. *Expect the unexpected* would be her new motto.

And the first unexpected thing she was going to do was convince a certain dark-haired devil that a good girl could be very, very bad.

Chapter Seven

Eric replayed the sentence in his head one more time just to make sure he'd heard it right. As much as he tried, no other word combination came close. His ears hadn't deceived him. His *abuela* had really just told Amara, "My *mijo* says you have the best *besos*."

They had stopped at the bakery on their way to the market. His mother had argued with his *abuela* that they didn't have time for a visit because they had a lot of errands to do on her only day off. But his grandmother had insisted the bakery's *pan dulce* was fresher and cheaper than the sweet breads at the market. Of course, he'd taken his *abuela's* side.

But now, as he watched Amara's face turn the same shade of pink as the bandana she wore on her head, he'd wished he'd agreed with his mother instead.

"He said what?" Amara asked, shooting him a couple of eye daggers. She probably thought he said something about the night of the baptism. He hadn't. Not a word, not to a soul.

But instead of saying anything in front of his mom and *abuela*, he pointed to the display case and the dome-shaped pastry and jam sandwiches rolled in coconut, which sat neatly stacked inside. Amara saw the "*kisses*" his *abuela* was referring to and her face returned to its normal caramel color.

"Are they *piña* or *fresa*?" she asked Amara, clapping her hands and bouncing like a kid about to get candy. He couldn't help but smile when Amara grinned at his *abuela*. He recognized that delighted sparkle in her eyes. No wonder she was so good at baking. She baked because she loved to make people happy.

"I only have strawberry," Amara explained. "I've never made them with pineapple before."

Abuela sighed. "Not many people do anymore. I used to eat them all of the time when I was pregnant with my Diana here. *Piña* is my favorite, but I like *fresa,* too." She smiled again. "*Por favor, dame tres.*"

"Are you sure three is all you want, *abuela*?" he asked. "It's my treat. Fill up the box!"

"She shouldn't eat that much sugar," his mother warned.

He didn't care. He loved seeing his grandmother so excited. "She can eat half of one in the morning and the other half after her lunch. It will be fine," he insisted. When his mother turned her attention to the free samples of cut-up pastries displayed on the opposite end of the counter, he lowered his head and whispered in his *abuela*'s ear, "Don't worry, you can also have one after dinner." Then he planted a big kiss on her cheek.

He looked up and saw Amara staring at him with an expression he couldn't quite describe.

"So Eric, what is it that you've been doing here at night?

I've only been in here a few times but I don't really see much difference." The suspicion in his mother's voice grated on his nerves. He tried to deflect his growing irritation by rolling his eyes at Amara and attempting a smile.

He opened his mouth but Amara jumped in. "He actually already fixed a lot of things in the kitchen for us. And he's replacing the molding and paneling in here this week, right Eric?"

His mother looked at him to answer. "Yeah, that's right," was all he said.

"The real work, like the painting and flooring, will be next. I'm sure you'll be able to notice a big change after that stuff is done. My dad tells me every day how impressed he is by Eric's work. Your son really knows what he's doing."

Eric nodded sheepishly at his mother, while his grandmother beamed with pride. Why Amara was rambling and gushing, he didn't know. It's not like he asked her to justify his work, or help him impress his mother. Still, he admitted, it had been nice to hear those things. Especially from her.

They left the bakery a few minutes later, his *abuela* very satisfied with her purchase of *besos, bolillos,* and corn muffins. He opened the passenger door of his mom's Toyota Corolla and helped his *abuela* inside. After shutting her door, he went to open his own when his mom said, "Amara's all grown up, isn't she?"

He stared at her across the roof of the car. "What do you mean by that?"

"Nothing. I guess I'm just noticing, that's all."

"Okay," he said with a shrug, and opened the door.

"She seems like a nice girl," his mother continued.

"She is. What's your point, Mom?"

"My point is that for her sake and the sake of your job, I hope the only *besos* that girl is giving you are the ones filled with strawberry. I know what I saw in there, and I'm just telling you to be careful."

He didn't say anything so she got into the car. He stayed outside, trying to push down his anger and frustration before making a scene in front of his *abuela*.

Why did she have to go out of her way to tell him that Amara deserved better? He didn't need reminding. So what if he constantly kicked himself for not taking her that night in the shed? What would've happened if he had? Would Miguel have ever agreed to meet him? Would he have ever offered him the remodel job?

He'd done the right thing for once in his goddamn life, no matter how badly he wanted to pin her against the nearest wall and kiss her senseless every time they were in the same building. He didn't need anyone telling him that he didn't belong with Amara.

He already knew it.

But on days like today, when she stood up for him and made him feel like what he did mattered, it was definitely harder to accept. He should at least thank her for the kind words.

Eric bent down and knocked on the car window. His mom rolled it down. "Yes?"

"I need to talk to Señor Robles about something. I'll be home later."

Before she could answer, he ran back inside the bakery in search of Amara.

He would say thank you and leave. Nothing more, nothing less.

Hopefully.

"I'll be out in a few seconds," he heard her yell when he walked through the door.

If he waited, he'd second-guess what he was doing. He headed from the empty bakery toward her voice and found her walking out of the kitchen's pantry with a stack of foam coffee cups.

"Eric. What are you doing back here?"

He answered by taking the cups out of her hands and setting them down on a nearby counter. He'd only planned to talk to her. But knowing they were alone and this close was more than he could stand.

"Screw being a decent guy." He threaded his hands through her hair and brought her lips to his. It should have only been a quick kiss—just enough to let her know how much her words had meant. But the longer he tasted her, the more he wanted to *keep* tasting her. He expected her to break the kiss any second, to tell him he'd had no right to say one thing and do another.

Until then, he'd take his fill.

He moved his hands from her head to her ass and grabbed hold. She moaned into his mouth and he grabbed harder. Maybe she deserved better than him, but he'd bet every dollar he'd ever made, no one else could make that sound come out of her.

"God, you make me so crazy when you moan like that," he said as he moved his lips to her neck.

"You make me crazy when you *say* things like that," she said on a sigh.

Crazy. That was the perfect word for what they were doing. What *he* was doing. He'd promised Miguel he'd stay away from Amara and he was pretty sure that meant not sticking his tongue down her throat or squeezing her nipple through her shirt. If someone walked in on them right now, he'd have hell to pay for defiling the neighborhood saint.

And he was flat broke.

He stole one last hard kiss and pulled her hands off his chest. "I'm sorry. I know I shouldn't have done that. But you're so goddamn sexy, sweetheart, I just couldn't resist."

"Then maybe it's time to just give in," she purred and put her hands on his shoulders. "It can be our little secret. I promise I won't tell."

He shook his head and took her hands off him for the second time. "That's not the point."

"Then what is?"

"You don't fit into my plan."

She frowned. "What plan? The remodeling plan for the bakery?"

"No, the do-over plan for my life."

She shook her head, obviously still confused.

"Move back home. Check. Get a job. Check. Screw my ex-best friend's sister? No way."

She put her hands on her hips and basically dared him not to look at her pouty lips. "I'm more than just your ex-best friend's sister, Eric."

"That's exactly the problem."

Then he turned around and walked away from her. Again.

Chapter Eight

Amara looked up just in time to see her mom charging across the street toward the bakery. It was Thursday, but it felt like a Monday. A really long and awful Monday. She'd already burned a tray of corn muffins and dropped a gallon of milk on the floor and it was barely nine in the morning. Thoughts of that last kiss with Eric had her head all screwed up. The last thing she needed was whatever it was that her mother was about to tell her.

"What is this I hear about you charging Señora Rios two hundred and fifty dollars for a cake!" Consuelo yelled as she came barreling through the front door. "We charge one hundred for a sheet cake. You know that."

Amara's stomach fell. "How—? Wait, did she call you?"

"Of course she did! Now tell me why on earth you would charge her so much for a sheet cake?"

"Because she didn't order a sheet cake. She decided on a three-tier cake with fondant."

"Fondant? *Qué es fondant*?"

"It's a thicker type of frosting. It requires a lot more work and time. That's why I have to charge her more."

"But Señora Rios is the president of the women's club at church! She is a longtime customer and we need to charge what we've always charged her before she decides to stop ordering all of her cakes from us."

Her mother turned on her heels and walked into the kitchen. Usually, that meant the conversation was over. Maybe it was Eric's kiss or the fact she'd been excited to work on a fondant cake again, but whatever it was, Amara had had it. She was done letting others tell her what to do — inside *and* outside the bakery. Her fists balled up and her chest tightened.

She decided that this time, the conversation wasn't over.

Amara followed her mom into the kitchen. "Two hundred and fifty is a fair price. A cake like the one she wants would normally cost her five or six hundred dollars somewhere else. And it's not like she can't afford it. The Rioses own properties all over town."

Her mother spun around. "Why are we still talking about this? I already told her you made a mistake and the price is one hundred dollars."

"But I didn't make a mistake." Amara put her hands on her hips and stood her ground. "*You're* the one making a mistake by charging people prices from the 1990s!"

"Amara!"

"I'm sorry, Mom, but it's true." She waved a hand at the aging appliances, the not-yet remodeled flooring. "This bakery is never going to start making money if you don't increase some of the prices. The cost of ingredients alone has gone up and we need to account for that. Otherwise…well, you know."

"I understand that you are trying to help, but have you ever owned your own business? That's right, you did. And what happened? It closed after only three months. So I think I'm the one who knows best here. I'll talk to your daddy about changing some of the prices, but that will be a discussion *we* have, and *we* will let you know what we decide. Don't forget that this is still our bakery."

Fury boiled from Amara's head to her toes. It took everything she had not to yell back. Not because she was a coward, but because she knew it wouldn't change anything. Her mother was right. It *was* her parents' bakery. Amara only worked there.

She gritted her teeth. "Whatever you say, Mom."

Consuelo didn't respond. There was no need. That was the only answer she would've accepted anyway. She walked into the pantry, took the box of salt, and left out the back door. After she was sure her mother wasn't coming back, Amara ran to the front and pulled Daisy away from the stack of *tortillas* she was pretending to fix.

"I need your help," she told her.

"I don't know, Amara. I mean, I totally support what you're trying to do here but *tia* Consuelo scares me. A lot."

"No, I don't mean help with the bakery. I mean help with Eric."

"Eric? What are you talking about?"

"You were right. I want Eric. I just didn't want to admit it because that would mean admitting that I'm not going after him because of my parents and everyone else. Well, I'm sick of other people telling me what I can or can't do with my life."

"Okay, but I still don't understand."

"I want you to help me seduce him."

Daisy hooted and then pulled her into a big bear hug. You would've thought she'd given her permission to sleep with him herself.

"I love a challenge," Daisy sang as she did a celebratory dance around the bakery.

"Ouch," Amara replied.

"Sorry, *prima*. I didn't mean it like that. You don't need a huge makeover or anything like that. He's already interested. Trust me, I know these things," she added when Amara opened her mouth to argue. "He's standing at the edge of the pool. All he needs is the sign from you that it's okay to jump in."

"But I already told him to jump in and sometimes he does but then immediately jumps right back out," she explained. "How can I get him to get over whatever it is that's making him stay away?"

Daisy shrugged. "Simple. Make it completely and utterly impossible for him not to give in to the temptation that is you. And if that still doesn't work, there's one trick us women have been using for centuries to get a man to fall to his knees."

"And what's that?"

"Get another man to do it first. In other words, make him jealous."

Five hours later, Amara looked at herself in the small

bathroom mirror and examined her newly cut bangs. Daisy had called her stylist and gotten Amara an appointment that same day. The salon had been fancier than the Supercuts she'd been going to for her regular trims. So she'd expected to pay a little more. But eighty-five dollars to cut less than two inches of her hair seemed a little ridiculous. Still, she had to admit she liked the way her new expensive bangs framed her face. Besides the trip to the salon, Daisy had also ordered Amara to go shopping and to come back to the bakery with some new outfits, shoes, and jewelry sets. Luckily, she'd approved all of her purchases and then left to go buy herself a pair of heels that Amara had found on sale.

She planned to show off her new haircut and her new "butt-popping" jeans (Daisy's words) to Eric when she paid him a visit later that night. She even had the perfect excuse. Last night, she had baked a special surprise for his *abuela*. Even now she smiled, thinking about the expression on his face when she showed him what she'd made.

Hopefully, the night would work out to be as perfect as she had planned. Her parents were going to have dinner with Trina, since Miguel was working late and, as of yesterday, she was officially overdue. Poor Trina. She'd become Consuelo's new project and Amara knew her mom was pulling out all the stops to ensure what she thought was her rightful place in the delivery room. That meant feeding and pampering Trina as much as Trina would let her. Amara figured she had at least three hours to implement her seduction plan. This phase included kissing. Lots of kissing.

Combining the cost of the ingredients for her extra baking projects and the cost of her handful of new clothes, plus the new bangs, Amara estimated her seduction of Eric totaled just over three hundred dollars. She'd almost reached the limit for her credit card. She could only afford to pay the minimum this month. It was the most she'd ever been in debt since her cupcake shop closed.

Seduction, it turned out, could be very expensive.

Looking at her reflection in the mirror, she told herself, "He'd better be worth it."

Jingle, jingle.

She blew up a breath that rustled her bangs. "I'll be right there," she called out, hoping this customer would buy everything in the bakery so she could run home and get ready for tonight.

But the sight of Eric standing at the counter called for a change in plans.

"Hey," he said.

"Hi," she told him back. He looked extra good to her. Something seemed different about him. It pulled her toward him as she came around the counter.

"Are you the only one here?" He moved closer.

"Yeah. Daisy just left, and the parents are heading over to Miguel and Trina's." Was it his hair? No. Was it his clothes? She didn't think so.

He took another step toward her. "Oh, is she…?"

"In labor? No, not yet." She studied him more. Something was definitely different. "Why are you here, Eric?"

What was it about him today that raised the tiny hairs along her arms?

"I came to see you. I needed to…" His voice trailed off as he studied her face. "Did you get a haircut?"

The heat rushed to her cheeks as she nodded. Bracing for his next words, Amara didn't expect to feel his fingers brush some strands from her cheek. His touch left an exquisite sear along her skin and she ached for more.

He wants you, Amara. That's what this is. Show him that you want him, too.

A few weeks ago, heck, even a few days ago, she'd try to make a joke in order to lighten the heaviness of the moment. Today, pure carnal lust overrode any lingering fear. She took a deep breath and walked past him to the front door. She lowered the shade on the window, turned the lock on the door, and then faced Eric.

"What are you doing?" he asked as she approached him.

"Giving you permission."

"Permission for what?"

"To do what you came here to do." This time, she reached out to touch him. His damp hair cooled her fingers as she threaded them through it.

"Goddamn it, Amara," he groaned and closed his eyes. "I came here to tell you that we couldn't kiss again but now all I can think about is kissing you again."

She waited for him to touch her in return, but he didn't. She was about to ask him what he was waiting for when the theme song to the movie *Halloween* started blasting from her pocket. She jerked her hand away.

Eric opened his eyes. "Your phone is ringing," he finally said.

"I know."

"Are you going to answer it?"

The ring tone alerted her to the very aggravating fact that it was her mother calling. Did she have some sort of Spidey-sense when it came to her daughter's hormones? But she refused to let Consuelo ruin this moment.

The phone quieted.

"It's just my mom. She'll leave me a message. Now, you were saying something about kissing me?"

He opened his mouth but his own phone interrupted him. He glanced at the screen. "It's your dad."

And just as she was about to tell him to let it go to voicemail, the bakery's phone started ringing, too.

Deep down she figured it was her mom again, but she couldn't take a chance in case it was a customer. She jogged to the cash register and answered the black cordless phone sitting on the counter. "Robles Panaderia, how can I help you?" she asked, trying hard not to unveil the irritation and frustration prickling at her skin.

"Amara!" her mother shrieked. "Why didn't you answer your phone?"

"I, uh, I was helping a customer," she lied. Across the room, Eric was on his own phone.

"Well, it's time! It's time! Trina is on her way to the hospital."

"Oh my gosh! Is she okay? Is Miguel okay?"

"Yes, they're fine. We're driving her right now. But we left in such a hurry that we forgot her bag at the house. I need you to go there and pick it up and meet us at the hospital."

"Right now?" She looked at Eric who had joined her at the counter.

"Yes, of course, right now. She needs her bag. Just close up the bakery and meet us at the hospital."

"All right, I'm on my way." The line clicked.

Eric had already hung up his phone. "Sounds like you're about to become a *tia*."

"Yeah, I guess so. Listen Eric…"

He put his hand up. "Your dad wants me to get some tarps from your garage. He says you have the key. Can I get that from you and I'll give it back after you get back from the hospital?"

"Don't you think we should talk?"

"No. I think you need to be with your family and I need to get those tarps."

The coolness of his voice deflated her. If he'd been thinking about kissing her before, he sure as heck wasn't now. And she wasn't about to throw herself at him only to get rejected all over again. She grabbed her keys from her pocket and shook them at him. "I have no idea which key it is, plus their garage is like an episode of *Hoarders*. I'll go with you."

"Fine," he said with a shrug.

"Fine," she said.

As she left the bakery, all she could think of was how *not* fine things had suddenly become.

· · ·

They said nothing as the crossed the street. Or as they walked up steps to the detached upper level garage located behind the Robles' main house. He still didn't know what had come over him back at the bakery. He'd been so close to giving in to his constant and unrelenting urges to take what she'd been trying to offer him.

Then he got the call from her dad. Like he told Amara, her dad had wanted him to get the tarps. But what he didn't tell her was that her dad had also decided that he wanted the remodel done in two weeks.

It had been the reminder he needed that anything with

Amara would only be temporary. He had to focus on getting his shit together. A good reference from Señor Robles could be just what he needed to get more jobs, which would lead to more money, and more connections to start his business back up. He had to keep it in his pants until he finished the bakery job.

Once they reached the top, he tried opening the padlock on the garage door with one key after another. "Your dad said they're going to be staying at Miguel's house for a few days and Daisy's going to stay here with you?"

Amara scoffed. "Not if I can help it. Just because I'm chained to the bakery doesn't mean she has to be."

He heard a *click* and successfully turned the key until the padlock popped open. She helped him raise the rolling door. What he saw made him laugh.

"You were right. This *is Hoarders*." The tiny one-car garage held no automobiles, but towers and towers of cardboard boxes, plastic tubs, and bursting garbage bags. It was… chaos. Luckily, the blue tarps he needed were near the front of the mess, folded neatly on a plastic lawn chair.

Amara rummaged through a cardboard box she'd somehow extracted from the cluttered mess. "Look what I found! It's stuff from when Miguel was in high school!" As she thumbed through papers, Eric noticed his senior yearbook. He pulled it out of the box and they moved closer together to take a look. He opened it to a photo that showed him, Miguel, Trina, and Mariah at some rally.

"Look at how skinny he was," said Amara, with a laugh. "Good thing he's not that skinny anymore. I mean could you imagine if he had a baby back then? He wouldn't even be able to carry it!"

Memories, painful ones, surged through Eric's head. He shut the book and threw it back in the box.

"Oh my gosh. I'm so sorry. I shouldn't have said that. Sometimes I forget, you know…" Her voice trailed off.

"That I was almost a dad," he finished her sentence. He didn't mean to sound so bitter, especially not to her. "It was a long time ago. It's fine."

"Do you ever think about it? I mean, the baby?"

A faded sense of loss tugged at his insides. He shrugged it away. "Not so much anymore. I mean I was sad when she lost it, but now I know that it was for the best. Besides I'm no one's role model, right?"

He laughed but Amara didn't look amused. "Why do you say things like that about yourself? You're not that bad."

"Yeah, that's what you think." He guided her out of the way so he could pull down the garage door and then handed her the keys.

"That's what I *know*. You've made some mistakes, we all have. So what? Get over it."

"It's not that easy, Amara, especially when people around here like to remind me every chance they get." He rolled the tarps under his arm and headed for the street.

"Why are you walking away from me?"

"I'm not walking away from you, I'm walking toward the bakery." They made it to the bottom of the stairs in one piece. Not a small feat, considering he was practically running down them. Once it was safe to turn around, he looked at her. "Why is it so important to you whether I'm bad or good?"

"Because I think it's time to forgive yourself and stop worrying about what others think of you."

She touched his arm, probably to soothe him. It only reminded him that he couldn't—shouldn't—touch her back. Bitterness stung at his throat. He let out a loud, sarcastic laugh. "Really? This is the advice you're giving me? Trust me, Amara. You don't want to have this conversation."

He darted across the street to get away from her before he said something he'd regret. His neck muscles tightened and his head pounded.

She'd forgotten to lock the door when they left so nothing stopped him from barreling into the bakery. He threw the tarps in the corner with his other supplies and spun back around, reaching for the door just as Amara pushed it open.

"You're in my way," he said.

She shook her head and crossed her arms. "I'm not moving until you tell me what you meant back there."

"Amara, please. I don't want to do this."

"I can see the vein on your neck throbbing. Just tell me why you're so angry!"

All of his frustration finally erupted. "Fine! I'm angry at everyone in this fucking town who thinks they're better than me. I'm angry that the only reason I have a job is because my former best friend begged his parents to give it to me. And I'm angry that his sister thinks she knows everything about me when, in fact, she doesn't know shit!"

She stepped to the side to let him pass. But he wasn't done. Not by a long shot.

"I can't believe you have the nerve to tell me that I shouldn't let others decide how to live my life when you're doing the same goddamn thing! Why are you here, Amara? Huh? I heard you had a fancy job and your own apartment back in Chicago, but now here you are, helping your parents and not making a single damn decision for yourself."

She looked away from him. "You don't understand. It's complicated."

"Bullshit! You're twenty-six and you still let your parents run your life."

"And what about you? You still live with your mom!"

"I had nothing in Vegas! Nothing! I had to come back. You had a life in Chicago and you chose to leave it. So don't compare my situation to yours. We're not the same."

"You know, Eric, in case you haven't noticed, I'm trying to be your friend. Maybe I should just stop trying so hard."

Her words gutted him. "I never asked you to be my friend. And since we're never going to be anything else, maybe it's time to put an end to this silly dance once and for all."

He grabbed her shoulders and moved her until her back pressed up against the bakery's door. Then he leaned into her, bracing his hands on each side of her body. His mouth hovered near hers, though he didn't kiss her. The wild look in her eyes and the flush of her face told him she was as turned on as he was.

It didn't matter. Not anymore.

"I'm not blind, woman, and I'm certainly not dead." He moved in closer, dragging his open mouth along her throat. Her gasp threatened to snap his control. "You've been doing your best to tempt me into finishing what we started the night of the baptism. I'll admit the last few times I've seen you it's taken everything I have not to push you into that pantry and fuck you senseless."

She arched against him and whimpered. "Eric..."

It'd be so easy to give in to what she wanted. What he

needed. Her nipples beaded, and even through the layers of clothes separating their bodies, the sharp points brushed against his chest. What he wouldn't give for a taste. No, more than taste. He wanted to *devour* her.

He stepped back and ran his hands through his hair and heaved out a breath. "But like I said before. You and me are a bad idea."

She sagged against the door, anger flaring in her eyes. "There you go again, telling me what you think is best for me. What about what I want?"

His hands dropped to his sides. "Exactly what is it that you want? A quickie in the pantry? A screw on the counter? I get that you want to fuck, but why, Amara? Why me?"

If his harsh words shocked her, she didn't let it show. She blew up instead. "Forget it!" she shouted, pushing off of the door and crowding him so that he had to take another step back. "I'm done throwing myself at you. You don't want me to be your friend. Fine. I'm not. You don't want to sleep with me. Fine. Don't. You're not the only *churro* in town."

He would've laughed if he hadn't been so pissed off. "And what the hell is that supposed to mean?"

"It means, I may not be all confident and sexy like the girls you're used—"

He dragged his eyes up and down her body. "I never said you weren't sexy."

"Yeah, well, all I'm saying is that I'm sure there's someone out there who would appreciate what I have to offer."

The muscles in his neck flexed tight at the thought of some random guy making her scream with pleasure like he had on the night of the baptism party. He needed to get away from her. If he didn't, he wouldn't be able to stop himself from showing her that he was the only man she needed.

He pushed past her and made for the door. "Do whatever you want—for a change. Just don't forget I'm painting tomorrow night so you're going to need to empty the refrigerator case before you leave for the day."

It was better this way, he told himself as he walked home. Finishing the bakery remodel had to be his top priority. And if he'd just lost whatever chance he'd had with Amara, then that was the price he had to pay in order to turn his life around.

Besides, Amara had never been his to lose.

Chapter Nine

"Oh my gosh it's so good."

Amara licked the spoon clean and sighed. Her new mango cream cheese frosting was the perfect pairing to her revamped coconut *tres leches* cupcakes. It was sweet, but not too sweet, creamy, and all kinds of buttery goodness. Surveying the two dozen beautiful creations before her, she couldn't help but be impressed with herself. Even the diced, candied mango squares she'd added to the tops at the last minute were ah-mazing.

Eric doesn't know what he's missing.

She meant the cupcakes, of course. After their argument yesterday, Amara had shelved her little seduction plan. For all his mixed signals, he'd made it perfectly clear that he was determined not to be with her. As she painstakingly arranged the little delights onto two pedestal cake platters inside the refrigerated section of the display counter, she tried not to think of him or his hurtful words. Sure, they had motivated her to finally try out the recipe she'd been thinking about, and perhaps he'd even pushed her into trying to sell the cupcakes today. What her parents didn't know…well, they didn't know.

On the self-standing chalkboard sign her dad used to advertise their homemade tamales during Christmastime, Amara carefully wrote:

TODAY'S SPECIAL
GOURMET COCONUT TRES LECHES CUPCAKES
WITH MANGO CREAM CHEESE FROSTING
$3 EACH OR $10 FOR 4

Then she waited. And waited. And waited some more.

Two hours later she'd sold a dozen plain *bolillo* rolls, about twenty dollars worth of assorted sweet breads and cookies, and a pack of corn *tortillas*. But no cupcakes.

After another hour and no cupcake sales, Amara went outside and wiped the chalkboard sign clean with a dishtowel. Then she wrote:

TODAY'S SPECIAL
COCONUT TRES LECHES CUPCAKES!!!!
WITH MANGO CREAM CHEESE FROSTING
$2 EACH OR $5 FOR 3

A sprinkle of customers came in, keeping Amara busy with sales of assorted Danishes and cookies. She even got a birthday cake order for the following Saturday. People looked at her cupcakes, but their eyes wandered away before she could even try out her sales pitch. By three p.m.

she still had twenty-two cupcakes sitting on the platter (two had been her lunch). Heaving a big sigh, she made her way out to the chalkboard sign:

TODAY'S SPECIAL!!!!
CUPCAKES!!!!!
$1

She shuffled back inside the bakery. The defeat weighed on her shoulders like five-pound sacks of flour. Pulling a chair out from the small table, Amara slumped down and put her head in her hands. Tears stung her eyes; disappointment quivered her chin. She didn't know what was worse — realizing that these delicious desserts were fated for the trash, or having to accept that her mother had been right after all: gourmet cupcakes had no place in East L.A. or the Robles Panaderia.

This is what you get for trying. This is what you get for dreaming.

It was all Eric's fault. If it weren't for his accusations yesterday, she would have never even tried. Anger rose from her belly, burning her throat as if she'd gulped down a handful of *jalapeño* seeds. She wiped away her tears and any remaining self-pity. How dare he try to analyze her or judge her? And why did she care so much about what he thought?

We're never going to be anything else. Those words had hurt before. Now they just made her mad. She rose from the table and stared at the cupcakes that mocked her from behind the glass. Part of her wished she could just shove them in Eric's face and down his throat. Maybe he'd even choke on a few of those candied mango pieces. He couldn't criticize her if he couldn't breathe, right? But despite her newly formed feelings of despise toward him, Amara thought better of using her baked items as weapons of revenge. So she headed to the kitchen in search of a trash bag.

Jingle. Jingle.

The first thing she saw when she turned around was a pair of Ray-Ban aviator sunglasses. The tiny designer logo spoke volumes about the man who just strode into the bakery. Combined with his expensive haircut, expertly groomed mustache and goatee, and crisp charcoal gray business suit, Amara knew he wasn't from the neighborhood. The only time anyone wearing a suit walked into the bakery was to pick up a platter of cookies for a funeral reception. She usually heard when a neighbor had passed away, and since there were no familiar names listed in last week's church bulletin, this mystery man was just that—a mystery.

"*Buenas tardes*," the man said, acknowledging her presence with a slight nod. He surveyed the perimeter of the bakery before walking up to the self-serve case of sweet breads, rolls, and donuts.

She noticed the large gold watch encircling his left wrist. He definitely had money. And Amara needed to make sure he spent some before he left to go back to wherever he came from. "*Buenas tardes*. Can I help you find something? I just pulled those *bolillos* from the oven so they're nice and warm."

"I can tell. They smell delicious."

So do you. She took another whiff of Mystery Man's subtle cologne or aftershave. Pleasantness tingled her nose.

He came over to the counter, took off his sunglasses and put his hands on the counter. "Although I'm sure those *bolillos* taste fantastic, I'm looking for some type of pastry or maybe a flan? I need to feed this sweet tooth of mine."

Mystery Man flashed a bright smile and Amara couldn't help but smile back. His hazel eyes sparkled as much as his perfect white teeth. "We have flan!" she exclaimed, maybe just a little too enthusiastically. With a wave of her hand that would rival Vanna White's, she showed him the refrigerated section of the counter. "And we also have rice pudding, *capirotada*—"

"What kind of cupcakes are these?" Mystery Man pointed through the glass to her cupcakes.

Amara's heart leapt. She couldn't believe she'd forgotten about them. "They're Coconut *Tres Leches* with a mango cream cheese frosting."

"Sounds good. Are these the ones on special for a dollar?"

While she wanted desperately to sell her cupcakes, she decided to take a gamble on what her gut—and that gold watch—told her.

"Oh, no, sorry. Those were the regular cupcakes. I actually just sold out of those. These are the gourmet cupcakes. They're three dollars each."

"Okay, I'll take one."

One cupcake only. She fought to keep her smile from collapsing and told herself it was still one more than she'd sold all day. So she smiled like a wild woman when Mystery Man handed her a five-dollar bill and kept on smiling as she handed him back his change. She slid open the small rectangular door to the refrigerated section and pulled out one of the more perfect-looking cupcakes with a pair of plastic tongs. She asked him if he wanted her to box it up.

"Nope. I'm going to eat it here right now. Don't want to

get crumbs in the Beemer, you know."

She actually didn't know but nodded like she did and then handed it over along with a napkin. He carefully unwrapped the bottom before taking a bite. She couldn't help but gawk as he chewed. He closed his eyes and nodded his head. Familiar anxiety tightened her chest as she watched Mystery Man consume the rest of the cupcake. He didn't say anything for several seconds. And she didn't breathe for that long either.

Mystery Man swallowed the last bite and wiped his mouth with the napkin. Then he opened his eyes.

"Did you make these…I'm sorry, I didn't get your name."

Her heart had been pounding so loudly in her ears that his words sounded muffled. Did he just ask her name? "My name is Amara, and yes I made the cupcakes."

His smile calmed her anxiousness. "Well, Amara, I have to tell you that was one of the best cupcakes I've had in awhile. My name is Brandon Montoya and I have a proposition for you."

• • •

Eric muttered under his breath as he emptied bottles of water and cartons of milk from the refrigerator case. He couldn't believe that Amara hadn't done it like he'd asked.

So what if they had argued. So what if he had turned her down…again. This was about her business and she should've helped him out.

He was already at least thirty minutes behind schedule and he still wasn't close to being done. Miguel was supposed to stop by on his way to the hospital and drop off some more cans of paint. Eric had hoped to have the case cleaned and moved before he got there.

The back door creaked open, signaling that he'd just run out of time.

"Hey man, sorry, but I'm not done cleaning the case yet. Your sister forgot to empty it before she left today," he yelled from the front of the bakery.

"I know. That's why I came back."

If the sound of Amara's voice startled him, then the sight of her just about knocked him over. She stood in the kitchen's doorway looking the damn sexiest he'd ever seen her. Her usual wild waves had been tamed into a new sleek and straight hairstyle and her face glowed, from the shimmer of bronze around her eyelids to her glossy pink lips. Eric swallowed hard, surveying her halter-style dress, which exposed bare shoulders and a teasing hint of her ample cleavage. The black sundress fit snug on top, but then flared from her waist into a flowy skirt embroidered with a swirling gold flower design. The dress fell just below the middle of her calves and he could see her perfectly polished red toenails peeking from her high-heeled sandals.

Desire pierced the shield he thought he'd built back up after their fight yesterday.

He clung to the carton of milk in his hand like his life depended upon it. Words escaped him. He wanted to tell her how beautiful she looked, and how much he so wanted to pull her into his arms and forget that he ever said they didn't belong together. As she stood there, not saying a word either, he told himself he'd wait for a sign. Something, anything, to let him know that she still wanted him as bad as he still wanted her. If she did, then he'd make her his that night.

She took a step toward him, and he started to move closer when a catcall whistle screeched from the shadows of the darkened kitchen.

"Look who's all dressed up!" Miguel entered the bakery and Eric froze in place. His friend walked to his sister, took her by the hand, and made her twirl in front of him. "Wowee, Amara! You look amazing!" The rosiness of her blush-covered cheeks deepened and Eric wished he could say something to put her at ease. She had nothing to be embarrassed about. She did look amazing.

"So what's the special occasion? Did you finally let mom set you up on a blind date?"

Miguel helped himself to one of the bottles of water Eric had just taken out of the case and stood next to him— both of them facing her.

"No. It's not a blind date," she looked at him, not her brother. "This guy came into the bakery today and he tasted one of my cupcakes—"

"You made cupcakes...to sell in the bakery?" he interrupted, finally finding his voice.

"I did," she said coolly. "Anyway, he loved it and apparently he owns this new restaurant downtown so he asked me to have dinner with him, you know, at his restaurant, and—"

"So it is a date. Good for you! What's his name?" This time Miguel interrupted her, which was fine with Eric since he didn't want to hear much more after she said the guy asked her to dinner.

"Well, it's..." She looked at him again, but he turned away to finish emptying the case. "His name is Brandon Montoya."

"Brandon Montoya," Miguel echoed. "That name

sounds familiar. Wait a sec, does he own a restaurant called L.A. Cuchara?"

Even Eric knew who Brandon Montoya was. Not because of his restaurant but because he'd just seen something on TV about the guy being named one of Hollywood's bad boy bachelors. The guy had a reputation for sleeping with, and then dumping, actresses and models. And now he was taking *his* Amara to dinner?

Rage swelled inside. He took it out on the next water bottle, throwing it harder than he needed. It missed the crate and bounced off the floor. Eric swore under his breath and picked it up without looking at either of them.

Amara and Miguel continued their conversation, not even noticing Eric's growing irritation. "Yes," he heard her say. "That's the restaurant I'm going to tonight. How did you know?"

"Our firm made a bid for his building. But his company ended up bringing in the same architects who built his New York restaurant," said an obviously impressed Miguel. "Dang, I can't believe my sister is dating a millionaire restaurateur."

"I didn't say I was dating him," she blurted, a little too quickly. Eric turned around. She met his stare for a few seconds before looking at her brother. "Well, this is our first dinner. Let's just wait and see how tonight goes before you start marrying me off, okay?"

They both laughed, but Eric didn't join in. The uneasiness in his stomach wouldn't let him even a crack a smile. "Excuse me, but I have to go get more crates," he mumbled. As he walked by Amara, he didn't dare look at her for fear she'd try to talk to him.

But just as he passed her, she said his name. He stopped but didn't turn around.

"I'm sorry I didn't empty the case like you asked. The excitement of everything, well, I guess I forgot. I was hoping I could do it tonight before you showed up. But then you were already here."

"It's fine," he snapped, betraying the angry swell of emotions raging in the pit of his stomach. He quickened his steps and walked out of the kitchen's back door, into the alley.

Pacing, he tried to regain his composure. Seeing her tonight in that dress and hearing about her date with a successful businessman had sent him stumbling into a place he hadn't been to in a very long time.

Eric Valencia didn't do jealous. If the girls he dated ever flirted—or more—with other guys he always ended things on the spot. He figured if they wanted something different then they could have it. Why waste his time? And it was always easy to let them go. He learned at seventeen that being invested in one person left him open to being used or hurt. He'd spent the last twelve years erecting a barrier around his heart to keep it safe from ever being that vulnerable again. And no woman had ever threatened to breach that wall. Until now.

You told her it was okay to find someone else.

True. But he hadn't expected her to find that someone in a day.

A familiar craving for his old friend Jack Daniels whet his lips as if he'd already taken a drink. He closed his eyes. He could feel his control slipping away. The last few days had been hard. He'd been so focused on battling his attraction to

Amara that he'd loosened the grip a little on his tether to sobriety. It would be so easy to bail for the night and walk to the nearest bar.

If you leave now, you know you'll never come back.

His own bluntness startled him. Yet it was the truth. His sponsor had once told him that alcoholics were the best liars in the world, especially to themselves. And only when you started being honest with yourself could you take responsibility for the decisions you made.

Eric knew he'd just come to a crossroads where what happened next could change his life forever. Did he really want to say, "Fuck it," and fall back into his old ways and old problems? Or did he want to take control of the situation and continue on this road to a redemption of sorts?

One path was definitely easier than the other. But it would also probably end with his *abuela* crying over his grave.

Eric paced the alley until the urge to drink passed and he knew he could walk back into that bakery and focus on the job he had to do. He'd go to a meeting tomorrow afternoon. Maybe he'd even call his sponsor later tonight.

He'd do whatever he needed to keep that drink out of his hand and Amara out of his head.

Taking one last deep breath, he picked up one of the plastic crates he'd come out to get and hurled it against the alley wall.

• • •

Rrrr Rrrr Rrrr Rrrr
Amara turned the key again.

Rrrr Rrrr Rrrr Rrrr

"Come on!" She slapped the steering wheel. "Come on Stella!" Her 1967 blue Ford Mustang flicked her dashboard and other interior lights in response. After a couple more tries, though, the lights went dark and she heard only a *click* when she turned the key again.

It was after ten-thirty and she was alone in her car in the parking lot down the street from L.A. Cuchara. She debated going back to the restaurant and asking Brandon if he knew anything about cars. But she remembered his stylish Armani suit and figured he probably preferred to stay away from a greasy engine. She could call her dad, but that would mean explaining to her mother why she was downtown in the first place, which would involve her spilling her surreptitious plan to sell the cupcakes. That left her brother. But after her fourth attempt to call only reached his voicemail, she figured he must be asleep or have his phone turned off so not to wake the baby.

You're a big girl, Amara. Just call a tow truck.

She looked around the almost deserted parking lot. Without enough cash for the restaurant's valet, Amara thought she'd lucked out finding a back corner spot in a lot on the same block. Now the shadows hid her car from the street—which meant they would also hide anyone trying to abduct or kill her. It wouldn't be the smartest thing in the world for her to meet a strange tow truck driver out here in the dark all alone. She needed someone with her, someone to drive her home in case the tow driver wasn't a serial killer but still couldn't get Stella started.

Biting her lip, she punched Eric's number into her cell phone. And an hour later she was in his car on the way back home, regretting her decision.

Silence erupted between them as soon as the tow truck driver left them standing in the parking lot of a family friend's repair shop. The friend had allowed her to leave Stella there and he'd check on her in the morning. He'd been a lot nicer about being disturbed so late at night than Eric. On the phone, Eric grumbled. As the tow truck driver worked, he sighed. Behind the wheel, he didn't say a word— just stared straight at the road ahead of them.

"Thanks again for coming to get me. I know I interrupted your work, so I appreciate you doing this."

Silence.

"Old Stella's been running pretty great lately, so this was totally unexpected. Otherwise I would have taken my dad's car downtown."

Still no response. She imagined crickets chirping.

"I hope it's something simple like a bad spark plug or dead battery. I really can't afford any major repair issue right now, you know?"

This time, he coughed. Her fingers gripped her purse tighter, and an uncomfortable warmth heated her cheeks and forehead. Only her mother could give her the silent treatment. And only because she'd often give it right back.

"What's your problem? I get it that this wasn't the way you wanted to spend your night, but you didn't have to come. You could've told me no."

"No, I couldn't," he said at last, his voice hard and cold. "You're my friend's sister, my boss's daughter—there was no way I was going to leave you stranded in a downtown parking lot in the middle of the night."

The fact that he'd rescued her because of some sense of

responsibility to others only infuriated her more.

"I would've found a way home. I'm a smart girl," she huffed.

"Yeah, if you're so smart why didn't you ask your new *boyfriend* to drive you home?"

"What boyfriend? What are you talking about?"

"Don't play dumb. I'm talking about Mr. Millionaire Restaurant Guy. So, what—was he too busy planning menus to make sure you were safe?"

She remembered what she'd said back at the bakery. It was true that Brandon had asked her to dinner, but it wasn't a real date like she'd let Miguel and Eric believe. He wanted to wine and dine her in order to convince her to apply to be his next pastry chef. His previous one had just decided to go back to New York. That was why he'd come into the bakery in the first place—he was on a scouting mission visiting local L.A. bakeries from Westwood to Boyle Heights. *I want authentic Latin desserts with a gourmet twist. And your style is exactly what I've been looking for*, he'd told her over their seared scallops and sweet corn salad. When she explained that she couldn't leave the bakery, he asked if she would consider making special gourmet dessert items just for his restaurant, which he could sell on Friday and Saturday nights.

Telling Eric the truth now would be embarrassing, so she let him hold on to his assumptions. "It's not like that between us. We just met, remember? And what's up with this attitude toward Brandon?"

He shrugged. "It's not attitude. I just question a man's character when he doesn't pick up a girl for their first date, that's all. Did he make you pay for your own dinner, too?"

"Uh, it's his restaurant. We didn't have to pay for

anything. Not even the bottle of wine." The disapproving shake of his head bothered her so she hastily added, "I only had two glasses and I didn't leave until I knew it was out of my system. And for your information, Brandon even offered to let me sleep it off in his apartment above the restaurant, but I was fine…" The second she said the words, she regretted them.

He slammed the steering wheel with his hand. She jumped. "What were you thinking even considering going to a strange man's apartment all alone?" he roared. "This isn't like you, Amara. You're usually more sensible than this."

His words bristled her. She hadn't been sensible in that shed. Or any of the times they'd kissed in the bakery. The anger that had festered since yesterday came flooding back. "Just who do you think you are? I'm not a little girl anymore, and you don't have to protect me. I already have a big brother for that!"

She turned toward her door and looked out the window. Good thing they were still on the freeway or else she might have jumped from the car just to get away from him.

"You may not look like a little girl, but you sure as hell pout like one."

They sat in silence until the car finally lurched to an abrupt stop in front of her house. Amara swung the door open. All set to make a dramatic exit, which would include a very hard door slam, she remembered what was sitting on her kitchen counter. Letting out a frustrated sigh that sounded more like a growl, she turned toward Eric.

"You have to come inside."

"I thought you were a grownup who didn't need protecting? I think you can handle an empty house just fine." He didn't even look at her.

"I have to give you something. It will take two seconds and then you can leave." She wasn't going to beg him. If he wanted to come in, he'd come in. Amara stepped out of the car and slammed the door behind her. When she reached the steps leading up to her front porch she heard more slamming, and work boots stomping behind her.

She unlocked her front door and pushed it open. She didn't bother turning on the living room light and instead headed straight for the kitchen to grab the plastic container from the counter. Amara took a second and exhaled. She could feel the adrenaline pulsing through her veins. Anger, hurt, shock—it was a fiery cocktail heating her from the inside out. She blew out another breath. Squaring her shoulders, Amara turned on her heel and walked back to the living room where she knew Eric waited.

The light from the kitchen dimly illuminated the room, casting enough light that she could make out his tense jawline and his hands clenched into fists by his side.

She pushed the container into his chest. "Here."

He took a step back, but didn't take it from her. "What is it?"

"It's for your *abuela*. They're *besos*."

Eric raised his eyebrows. "I don't…"

She pushed the container farther into his chest. "They're *besos* filled with pineapple. You know, the ones she mentioned the other day." He continued to look at her, his eyes blank. Amara didn't understand why he wasn't understanding her. "Oh. My. God. Just take the darn thing!"

This time he took the container. She turned to walk away but stopped at the sound his voice.

"The *besos* with pineapple. You made them just for her?"

Amara turned back around and sighed. "Yes. I tried out a new recipe. Let her know that I wasn't sure how sweet she wanted the pineapple so they may not even be what she's used to. It's a trial batch."

"Why did you do this?" The biting, judgmental tone from before had disappeared. His voice was calm, almost soft. He raised his eyes from the plain, plastic box. The intensity of his gaze, even in the low light, nearly knocked her off her feet. She shifted her weight and crossed her arms.

"I...uh, well, she mentioned how much she loved them and, well, it really wasn't a big deal..." Why was she suddenly tongue-tied? "Like I said, she may not even—"

He dropped the container onto a nearby armchair, placed his large, rough hands on either side of her head, and crushed his mouth against hers. Fire, hot and searing, exploded throughout her body. Amara whimpered as his tongue urgently pushed her lips open.

"*Aye, Amara.* Sweet, sweet Amara," he whispered against her mouth.

Then his lips were gone.

Amara opened her eyes in protest as Eric untangled his hands from her hair. He grabbed his own head and backed away from her. "I'm sorry. I'm so sorry. I shouldn't have done that."

She sqeezed his arm before he could leave. "I'm not sorry."

"You know we can't...we shouldn't."

She *did* know. She knew she should just tell him good-night and send him on his way. She knew what could happen if she didn't. She knew all those things and still she didn't care. So she shrugged. Amara couldn't stop this even if she wanted to.

But he still could, and she saw the hesitation in the squint of his eyes. Amara knew she had to be forward. Time for her to speak up and tell him what she really wanted before he changed his mind. No, before she changed hers.

"I want you, Eric. I don't care about what happens next or what it means tomorrow, because it doesn't have to mean a thing. Just be with me tonight."

Pure desire gave her the courage she needed to make her move. She reached for his hand.

He took it, clasping his fingers around hers. Then she led him down the hall to her bedroom.

She walked backward through the door, still holding his hand. He pulled her close again and gave her a kiss. His lips were soft, his breath sweet. Her body hummed in anticipation of everything to come. She broke their kiss and slid out of her sandals while he sat on the edge of her bed and worked quickly to untie his boots. When he stood up, she reached up behind her in search of the dress's zipper.

"Let me do that," he said, pulling her hands down to her side and moving behind her. He untied the halter straps behind her neck, then touched the zipper. She nearly jumped out of her skin when she felt his soft lips on her back.

"Tell me something," he rasped. "Did you wear this for him? Your answer will determine how I take this dress off of you."

A thrill ran up her body. She tried to answer, but she could barely breathe.

He moved his lips to the side of her neck, just below her jawline, making a delicious trail of light, butterfly kisses that electrified every nerve. When he reached around and started caressing her breasts, she moaned in satisfaction.

"Well, I'm waiting. Am I going to rip this dress right off you so you can never wear it again, or am I going to slide it off your body using only my teeth?"

Her thighs quivered at his sexy threat. Either way sounded absolutely wonderful. She tried to regain some sense of control so she could answer. "I didn't wear it for him because it wasn't a date," she admitted, scared and excited about what he'd do to her for letting him think it was. "He just wants me for my baking skills, to work in his — "

More words escaped her as she felt him pull the zipper down with his teeth. Her breasts strained against her black lace bra, the friction hardening her nipples. When the dress finally fell to the floor, Eric's mouth traveled up her body. Her knees buckled when she felt something wet and hot against the back of her thighs.

She groaned. And when he licked her, just along the seam of her thong panties, she groaned even louder. Eric's mouth on her skin was beyond anything she could've ever imagined. Heat flared wherever he touched her, however he touched her. She wasn't just melting. She was combusting.

He moved his hands over her strapless bra, cupping her breasts and pinching her nipples into hardened peaks beneath the fabric. She curled into him, delighted by the hardness she felt behind her. Still, she needed to touch him the way she'd always dreamt of.

She turned in his arms and pulled his head down for a kiss. They tasted each other all over again—reveling in finally being able to feed their hunger. She explored his mouth, eventually settling on his bottom lip with light, playful nibbles and licks. He groaned and seized her mouth one more time before she broke away. Although the kissing was wonderful, she couldn't wait any longer, and began to lift his shirt. He took over, dragging the material over his head, so she focused on his belt buckle. With shaky hands, she pushed his jeans down. He stopped her, though, when she hooked her fingers in the waistband of his tented boxer briefs.

Oh no. Had he changed his mind again?

He put his forehead against hers. "Damn. I don't have a condom. Damn. Damn."

Relief made her smile. She kissed his nose, then went to her dresser and reached behind her mirror to the small box of condoms she'd carefully taped against the back. He arched an eyebrow and she laughed. "What can I say? I guess I had my hopes that they'd come in handy one day. And as for taping it behind my mirror, I learned a long time ago never to hide anything in easily accessible spots. Consuelo has 'accidentally' discovered things before."

He took the box from her and threw it on the nightstand next to her bed. Heat flared in his dark eyes. "Lie down, Amara."

The realization she was about to see Eric fully naked, and that he was about to see her, left her trembling. All of her teenage fantasies were coming true. Part of her wanted to slow things down so she could remember every detail. The other part just wanted him inside her already.

She obeyed his order and waited. When he finally pulled down his briefs, she sighed. She'd seen penises before, but Eric's was the first she'd describe as beautiful. It jutted out from his body as if it was calling out for her to touch it. To taste it. She licked her lips.

Eric knelt on the bed and slid in next her. He touched her cheek before finding her mouth again. As their tongues danced, she clutched his shoulder and back, desperate to feel his bare skin against hers. She guided his hands to her breasts and he expertly freed them from her bra. But when he started to pull down her panties, she decided it was time for another admission.

"I have to tell you something," she said as he kissed her neck. "I haven't been...I'm not that experienced."

"Neither am I." She felt his smile against her shoulder.

"I'm serious. I haven't had certain things done to me."

He moved his face above hers and looked into her eyes. "So, no one has ever..."

Both of them looked down the length of her body.

"No," she admitted, her voice thick and hoarse. "I've only been with one other man—my ex-boyfriend in Chicago. And, well, he wasn't very, um, adventurous." Although she wanted to turn away and not have to see the shock in his eyes, she couldn't. But there was no shock or judgment, only desire.

He touched her cheek. "I don't want to do anything that makes you uncomfortable. So you're going to have to tell me what's okay and what's not okay."

She nodded and he brushed his lips against hers in a soft kiss. He pushed himself up onto his knees and lifted both of her legs toward the ceiling. Inch by inch, his fingers pulled her black silk panties off of her. He brought her legs back down and stared at the vee between them. "Beautiful," he whispered. He straddled her then and leaned down to her breasts. The pressure of his cock against her entrance left her tingling and wanting more. She moaned in desperation.

"Do you want me to suck your nipples?" he asked, still teasing her with small licks near her rigid peaks. It was a beautiful agony. "Remember, you have tell me what you want."

His tongue proved to be a more than skillful tool and she ached—*ached*—to feel more of it. "Yes," she said with a heavy breath. "Yes, suck my nipples." He rewarded her command by taking one into his mouth and sucking it with a vigor that made her pant and squirm. She'd never been so turned on in her life.

After thoroughly savoring and licking both breasts, Eric moved off her and made his way down the bed. He lifted her legs again, one in each hand, and parted them. Still on his knees, he kissed one ankle and then looked at her. "Are you ready?"

Was she? Eric Valencia was about to do something to her no man had ever done before. She should've been apprehensive, even rethinking everything that happened so far. But when she looked into eyes, they reflected her own desire. No, she wasn't ready. But that didn't matter anymore.

Amara nodded to let him know she wasn't going to stop him. Ever.

He kissed her other ankle and then bent her legs at her knees. "Tell me what you want." He kissed the inside of her right thigh and it quivered back.

"I…I want you," she rasped.

He kissed her inner left thigh and she squeezed her comforter for dear life. "No, tell me what you want me to do."

A gush of air hit between her legs and she gasped. She was absolutely sure her comforter must be in shreds now.

"That was only my breath, Amara. Imagine how it's going to feel when it's my tongue on that hot, sweet pussy of yours. Just say the words. Tell me to lick you. Tell me to suck on your clit. And I will because I fucking want to taste every part of you. "

His crude words should've shocked her. Instead, they ignited her.

"I..," she started, but couldn't finish because he'd plunged a finger deep inside her. Her hips bucked and her toes flexed. Her body came alive. She needed to feel his tongue on her immediately. No more imagining. It was time to feel it for real. "I want...I want you to lick my clit...now!"

He answered her by flicking his tongue against it and she gasped. His tongue was warm and soft against the trembling bundle of nerves as he teased it with long, languid circles. When she was absolutely sure she couldn't take much more, he switched gears and sucked on her clit earnestly, all the while still thrusting one finger inside.

I'm going to die. The pressure building within her was beyond anything she'd ever experienced with her old boyfriend—or even with herself. The coming explosion would surely stop her heart.

Death by orgasm? So worth the risk.

Lick. Suck. Thrust. Lick. Suck. Thrust. Eric's mouth and fingers not only drove her mad with lust, they took her to the edge.

Amara moved her hands over her breasts, cupping their fullness and pinching her nipples. As a delicious tightness spread throughout her body, a soft moan—or maybe it was a groan—escaped her lips.

"Holy shit, Amara. That's the hottest thing I've ever

seen." Her eyes flew open and she discovered Eric staring at her from between her legs. She should've been embarrassed having been caught touching herself like that, but the hungry, wild look in his eyes merely fueled her desire.

"Please. Don't. Stop," she pleaded. He returned to his post, applying more pressure to the long, hot strokes against her swollen clit. Another finger penetrated her, thrusting hard against her inner walls. A wave of sheer ecstasy dragged her by her fingernails from any final shreds of modesty or self-consciousness. Breaths became sighs. Sighs became gasps.

"Oh. My. God. Oh. My. God," she moaned, shaking her head back and forth across her pillow. Her skin burned, her nerves tingled, her body hummed.

The explosion was imminent. All she needed was. One. More. Thing.

"Let go, Amara. I want to see you come."

The raw neediness in his voice sent her over the edge and straight into glorious destruction. Through a haze, she felt him move next to her and she rode out the final contractions curled onto her side and wrapped in his arms.

When the waves finally stopped, Amara leaned against him. She had survived the crash. Just barely. The tinny taste on her tongue told her she must have bitten her lip when she tried to stifle the scream that broke from her throat when her orgasm hit. Tears welled just beneath the rim of her eyes.

Don't be the girl who cries after sex!

She couldn't help it though. She always cried when emotion—any emotion—overwhelmed her. She had happy tears, sad tears, and even mad tears. These, however, were "holy moly that was amazing" tears.

Eric turned her so he could see her face, but his satisfied smile disappeared when he met her eyes. "What's wrong?" He touched the wetness below the corner of her eye.

"Nothing's wrong. I promise." She raised her head and kissed him. "That was amazing and…unexpected. Thank you."

He seemed to believe her assurances. "Don't be thanking me just yet. I'm not even close to being done with you."

• • •

Never in his wildest dreams would Eric have thought that one day he'd be having sex with his best friend's sister. He was pretty sure the thought had never crossed her mind either. Yet there they were in her bed, the line between friends and lovers not just crossed, but pretty much obliterated.

He moved on top of Amara, careful to keep his full weight off of her as he kissed away the tears from her cheeks. Her emotion surprised him. Was she really okay with what they'd just done? What they were about to do together?

No looking back, he told himself as he moved his kisses from her face and neck to her soft lips. He reached out and fisted her hair, deepening their kiss, but it wasn't enough. He was desperate to be in her. A part of her.

"Fuck, Amara! I want you so bad," he growled.

"Then take me."

It was all he needed to hear.

Eric leapt from the bed to cover himself with a condom from the nightstand. His dick was so hard it bordered on painful. But while he couldn't wait for release, he also wanted to make the experience last.

He climbed back on top of Amara and looked into her kind, trusting eyes once more for permission. She gave it to him not with words, but by reaching for his hand above her head and locking her fingers with his.

Sliding his cock inside her to the hilt, he was nearly blown away by her heat and tightness. It felt beyond words. So much so that he stilled—needing to take a moment so he didn't explode right then. When he found some control, he began to move.

Her breasts rubbed against his chest as he drove into her, as if to remind him they needed attention, too. He removed his hand from hers to brace himself on both of his forearms. This position gave him much better access to her breasts and he took full advantage until the room filled up with a frenzy of groans and ragged breaths. She met every one of his powerful thrusts, taking him deeper and clawing at his shoulders to make him pump harder. The sound of skin smacking against skin filled the room, spurring his climax toward a shattering conclusion. But he needed to take her with him. He adjusted his position to kneeling and moved her ankles from around his waist to his shoulders. Reaching between their bodies, he rubbed her clit.

"Eric!" The sight of her coming undone right before his eyes sent him hurtling into his own release. His body shuddered as he unleashed himself into her clenching pussy.

When he was sure he was completely drained, he fell off her and rolled to the side to reach for a tissue from the box on the nightstand. He wrapped up the condom and tossed in the wastebasket next to her bed. Then he collapsed next to her, both of them still trying to catch their breath.

"So…" she said after a few minutes.

"So?"

"That was…"

"Fan-fucking-tastic." It was the only word that came to mind. And it fit perfectly.

"I agree. In fact, I agree so much that I kind of want to take back what I said before."

"Okay." Truth was he didn't remember much after the first time she'd sucked his tongue. "I'm sorry. Remind me again what you said?"

"About this not having to mean anything."

"Oh. That." Of course it meant something. It meant consequences if anyone found out. First of all, he'd be jobless. He had broken the promise he had made to Miguel about staying away from Amara. He'd be friendless, too.

"Are…are you starting to regret it?" she finally asked.

He heard the anxiousness in her voice. "Are you?" Could she hear it in his?

"I asked you first."

He closed his eyes and it all came back to him in an instant. The feel of her. The sound of her. The taste of her. Eric turned on his side so he could look at her. But she kept her eyes focused on the ceiling. "No, I don't regret it," he told her truthfully and reached for her hand.

Small fingers clasped his. "Good. Neither do I. That's why I'm thinking that we should do it again."

She rushed out the last part and that made him smile. His cock jerked to attention. "Sounds good to me. I'm ready to go."

"What?" Her head turned toward him so he could see her surprised expression. "Really? So soon? Well, I didn't necessarily mean right now. I meant, like, tomorrow or the next day."

"So you're saying you want us to keep having sex?"

"Yes."

He grinned. "Amara Robles, are you asking me to be your boy toy?"

She socked him in the arm and he laughed. "No, of course not. I could never use someone for sex…only. How about we call our arrangement more like friends with benefits?"

He pushed up onto his elbow. "You have my attention. So, exactly how long would these benefits last? Is there an expiration date?" He tried to sound casual, but the dread that twisted his gut surprised him.

She frowned at the ceiling. "I don't know. I guess until one of us wants out? That, or until the remodel is done. I'm sure we won't be seeing as much of each other after that anyway. It just seems natural to stop things then. Well, the sexual things, at least." She turned to him and smiled. "We can still be friends, of course."

Eric wasn't sure how to respond. He'd never had a girl set the end date of a relationship in advance. He'd also never been with a girl who didn't want more than he was willing to give. A friends with benefit situation would be the best of both worlds. He'd be a fool not to say yes.

So that's exactly what he did before showing Amara that he was serious about being ready to go at it again.

Chapter Ten

Daisy walked around her like a lion circling its prey.

"I already told you, it's the bangs." Amara blew them off her forehead in attempt to make her point.

"It's not the bangs. It's something else." She tapped her lips. "I can see it on your face but I can't quite put my finger on it."

Amara bent over the pan of cupcakes that needed frosting, trying not to smile as images from the past two nights she'd spent with Eric flitted through her head. Her cousin hadn't seen her in a few days, so as soon as she'd walked in that morning, Daisy had insisted there was something different about her. Sex with the man of her dirtiest fantasies did that to a girl.

"Why are you smiling?"

Amara nearly dropped the chocolate cupcake she'd been inspecting. "What? I'm not smiling."

"You were just a second ago. You're happy about

something. Your face is glowing, you're smiling like an idiot, and I could swear I heard you humming earlier. What gives?"

"I like how this batch of cupcakes turned out. That's all."

Daisy folded her arms across her chest and cocked an eyebrow.

"Okay, fine. I'm happy. What's the big deal?"

"No, you're not just happy. You're, like, over the moon happy. Why? Did something happen with the bakery? Did your parents decide they were going to go live permanently with Miguel and Trina?"

"Ha! Yeah, right." Amara laughed, and this time she didn't care if her smile came back. She couldn't help it.

"Then what else would make you so happy that—" Her eyes widened. "Oh my God. You slept with Eric!"

Amara froze.

"That's it, isn't it? You had sex with Eric! That's awesome, Amara. Good for you!"

Daisy whacked her on the back and Amara dropped the unfrosted cupcake onto one of the perfectly frosted final products. Darn it. She sighed. She wanted to deny the truth about her and Eric, make up some excuse as to why she was so full of joy that morning, but she couldn't think of anything else.

So she admitted it.

"I did, but you have to swear not to say anything!"

Daisy grinned. "Of course, cousin. Your naughty secret is safe with me. I just need to know one more thing."

"What?"

"How was it? I guess it had to be pretty good because you're walking around here grinning like a cat who just swallowed the biggest mouse she ever had. Should I take that as you really did swallow the biggest—"

"Daisy!"

Her cousin pouted. "Fine. Keep the details to yourself, party pooper. So what does this mean? Are you guys together, like a couple?"

Amara shrugged, picking at the rainbow sprinkles dusting the ruined cupcake. "We decided we're going to keep it casual. No strings. That's why nobody else can know, okay? We're friends with benefits."

Daisy's eyes widened. "Wow, I'm impressed. You're using a hot guy just for sex." She nodded. "Nice."

Amara frowned and leaned against the counter. "I'm not using him. We're just two adults who decided we like having sex with each other so we're going to keep doing it until…"

"Until what? Someone gets a better offer?"

She bristled at the thought of someone else seducing Eric into her bed. "No, until we decide we want to move on, or until he finishes the remodel."

"Hmm, that sounds very uncomplicated to me," Daisy said. "Sex is usually *really* complicated."

"I guess it depends on the people." Amara turned back to the cupcakes. Their arrangement would work as long as she and Eric accepted the fact that it would eventually end.

"Well, I'm happy for you. Maybe I should go out and find someone to have uncomplicated sex with, too."

"If that's what you…wait, what? No, that's not what you should be looking for."

"Why not? It looks like it's making you happy, right?"

Was she happy? Remembering Eric's lips on her neck and his hands on her breasts *did* make her smile. "I guess what I'm saying is that this is what makes me happy right *now*. Maybe in two weeks or two months, it won't anymore. But I don't know if I would want this for you. You shouldn't be looking for someone to make you happy for a night or two. You should look for someone to make you happy forever."

"What about you?" Daisy asked. "You deserve forever, too, don't you?"

"I don't know. Maybe. But I have other things going on that are more important to me right now than finding someone who will make me happy for the rest of my life. That's why this thing with Eric works, I guess. It's hard to explain. Maybe I just want to be bad for once?"

Daisy snorted. "I get it. You want to rebel a little. That makes sense. Especially with your family."

You've got that right. Amara smiled. "Let's get back to work, okay? Johnny Bautista's sixth birthday party isn't going to cater itself."

The bakery descended into a comfortable silence, punctuated by Daisy's occasional curse when her frosting didn't come out as cleanly as she'd like. But despite doing what she loved, the longer they worked, the more Amara's smile faded.

Did she deserve forever?

When she was younger, she thought she did. Then she went all four years of high school without a single date. She didn't even have her first kiss until she was seventeen, and that was with a friend of a friend who turned out to be gay. In college she had a handful of first dates, but not many seconds or thirds. Then she met Martín after she moved to Chicago. She had just landed a job working as a pastry chef trainee at the five-star San Regis Hotel. He worked as a desk clerk in the hotel. They had sex on their fourth date, and if he noticed she was a virgin, he didn't say. She'd been grateful to get it over with and didn't even care if he called her again, but he did. And he kept on calling.

That's when she started to let herself believe that what they had could be forever.

After all, they seemed perfect for each other. They each came from the same kind of family, grew up in the same kind of neighborhood, liked the same food, and read the same kind of books. They never really fought, but the lack of fireworks in the bedroom made her doubt the relationship. After six months together, she figured she could learn to live with it if it meant she didn't have to spend the rest of her life alone.

Then one day Martín met her after a Friday night dinner service and told her he wanted to see other people. He told her she was a good woman and would probably make a good wife, but he wasn't ready for that kind of commitment. In fact, he didn't even know if he wanted to get married — ever.

Although she'd been devastated at the time, the breakup had given Amara the push she'd needed to apply for the pastry sous chef position at the resort — the one she eventually resigned from in order to come back home.

She huffed at the memory. "Forever" was overrated. She wanted fireworks instead. And Eric gave her that. Every single time.

Just thinking of him made her tingle all over. Or was that the sudden vibration of her cell phone in her pocket? Probably both. And when she looked at the caller ID and saw Eric's name on the screen, the tingles got stronger.

"What are you wearing?" he asked before she even said hello.

"An apron and—"

"And please say that's all."

She laughed and glanced down at her full-length jeans. "I don't think the county health department would appreciate me wearing only an apron when I serve customers baked goods."

Amara looked up just in time to see her cousin's jaw drop and blue frosting squirt across the counter, entirely missing the cupcake Daisy had been holding in her hand. Normally she'd be embarrassed. Not today.

"The county health department hasn't seen you naked," Eric continued. "I have, and I can say from experience that I would appreciate your lack of clothing very much."

She could feel her goofy smile from coming back. "So am I supposed to ask what you're wearing now?"

"You don't have to, but I'll tell you. I'm completely naked."

"Okay."

"I'm serious. I'm fisting my cock and imagining I'm inside you. But I don't want to imagine anymore. I want the real thing. Come over. Now."

She closed her eyes. The mental image of Eric doing what he said turned her on more than she thought it would. She never thought she could get into phone sex until him. He had a way with words, that was for sure. And those words were pebbling her nipples as if it were thirty degrees inside the bakery, not eighty.

Afraid Daisy would mangle even more tubes of frosting if she heard the rest of their conversation, Amara walked into the kitchen and whispered into the phone, "And what? I'm supposed to show up on your doorstep and announce to your mom and *abuela* that I'm there to have sex with you?"

"They're not here. Today's Mom's day off. They left a few minutes ago to go visit my mom's cousin all the way in Temecula. They're going to be gone for hours."

Now, she was really considering it.

He continued to try and convince her. "Come over and I'll make you come. I promise. I've already decided that I'm going to take you from behind today. That way I get a nice view of that beautiful ass while I'm sinking my cock into your tight pussy."

Warmth rushed to all parts of her body, and she leaned against the sink for support. Yep, she was a sucker for the dirty talk. Who knew? Yet it wasn't enough to make her drop everything.

She cupped her hand over her mouth and the phone. "I don't know, Eric. It's in the middle of the afternoon…"

"Haven't you ever heard of an afternoon delight?"

"That's what that means?"

Eric's laugh was so loud she had to pull the phone away from her ear. "Be here in ten minutes. And think of something new you want me to do to you."

"Uh, I think you seeing me naked during the middle of the day is all the new I can handle right now."

He didn't laugh this time, just sighed. "*Aye*, Amara, you are one of a kind, you know that? I've never been with anyone like you."

She wasn't sure if she wanted to know what he meant by that. But she asked anyway. "Is that a bad or good thing?"

"Oh it's good. It's very good." The husky tone of his

voice sent shivers down her spine. "Now you have nine minutes. See you soon."

The line clicked.

Only nine more minutes until she'd be in his arms again. Only nine more minutes until she would feel his mouth on her skin and his hands all over her body.

She threw off her apron and asked Daisy to cover for her. As she walked/ran to Eric's house she didn't care whether her cousin knew she was ditching work to have sex in the middle of the day. All she cared about was getting to Eric's as fast as possible.

And seven minutes later, she was in heaven.

• • •

"So, would you say that was delightful?"

It sounded more like a purr than a question to him. Eric looked over at Amara, who was lying next to him. She, too, was out of breath and wearing only a giant, satisfied smile.

"No, I'd say that was fucking amazing," he told her truthfully.

She looked at the ceiling and exhaled. "Yes, yes it was."

From the moment their lips met that afternoon, their need to be together was frantic and crazed. He had worried that Amara might need some more convincing to get her into his bed in the middle of the day, but she was just as hot for him as he was for her. She didn't even hesitate in telling him when she was ready for him to enter her. And when he did, it was like they both couldn't get him deep enough.

A burning sensation on his back told him they'd reached new heights that afternoon. He reached for her across the bed and pulled her to his side. She rested her cheek on his chest. "I think you scratched me this time," he said after kissing the top of her head.

She looked up at him, surprise and guilt in her eyes. "Oh my gosh. I'm so sorry."

He shrugged. "Don't be. I like being marked by you. It's a sign of you taking control when we're together."

"How? It's more like I lose control, isn't it?"

He combed his fingers through her hair. "Well, in a way because you're not worried about leaving a mark afterward. But when you're digging your nails into my back it's because you're pulling me into you—you're taking control of the rhythm. Does that make sense?"

She sighed. "Too bad I can't act like that in real life."

"What do you mean?"

"It's getting easier for me to tell you what I want you do to me here. Out there, it's not so easy."

"Like with your parents and the bakery?"

"Yeah. Remember that day when you told me I was living their life?"

The memory of their argument still stung. "I'm sorry. I should've never said that."

"Why? You were right. I did give up my life in Chicago to come here to help them save the bakery. But all I'm doing is exactly what my dad was doing before he hurt his back. Business is still slow. Now they might even lose the house if things don't turn around. So me giving up my dream and moving back here will have been all for nothing."

"Hey, look at me, sweetheart." She scooted up until she was inches away from his face. He turned onto his side and raised her chin with one finger. "I'm going to ask you a question and I want you to answer me honestly, okay?"

When she nodded, he continued. "Do you really want to run the bakery? And I'm not saying just work there—I'm talking about taking a real ownership of everything from the menu to the entire management of it?"

She took a second and then answered. "I do and I don't. I'm afraid."

"Afraid of what?"

"Of failing again."

"What do you mean?"

She flopped back onto her back with a sigh, her arm over her eyes. "Two years ago, I borrowed money from my parents to open up a cupcake shop downtown. They both warned me that no one would want to go to a bakery that only sold cupcakes, but I begged and pleaded and eventually they gave me the money. By the first month, I knew I was in over my head, but I was determined to do it on my own so I pretended business was great…until I couldn't pretend anymore. I had to close the shop and admit they'd been right. I had no idea what it took to run a business."

"What about now?"

She rolled over to face him. "I don't know. Part of me thinks I might be able to really do something with this place. Brandon is serious about selling my desserts in his restaurant. It would be huge for the bakery. I'm kind of excited about making it happen."

"Then tell them, Amara. Tell them what you want to do."

"And what if they say no?"

"Then you tell them you're going to do it anyway."

Her eyes grew big. "I don't know if I can."

"Sweetheart, less than hour ago you didn't think you

could have sex in the middle of the day. But you did, didn't you?"

"That's because you did it with me."

"Then I'll do this with you, too. Let's expand the remodel—do even more to make it into what you want it to be. I'm serious. If revamping the bakery is your new dream, then I'm going to help you build that dream with my bare hands."

He'd never meant anything more in his life. He honestly wanted to help her. And if it resulted in extending their arrangement for a few more weeks, that was icing on the cake. Pun intended.

She opened her mouth as if to say something, but instead kissed him hard. Moving her hand to the back of his head, she pulled him closer, deepening the intensity of their kiss. She finally broke away after a minute or so, leaving him just as breathless as before.

Then she took his right hand, which had been resting on his side, brought it up to her face and brushed her lips and the tip of her tongue against his palm. His cock, already awakened by their deep kissing, rose to full attention.

Smiling, she looked into his eyes and moved his palm between her legs. "I accept your offer, but I think there's something you need to do with these hands first."

Chapter Eleven

L.A. Cuchara lacked the hustle and bustle of the last time Amara had been there. With two hours before it re-opened for dinner, the square tables with traditional Mexican *talevera* tile designs sat empty. Crisply folded white linen napkins perched atop gleaming blue plates, while the silverware caught the soft glow of light from the hand-blown glass fixtures hanging overhead. Brandon had tried for a mixture of color and elegance, he'd said, and as far as Amara was concerned, he'd knocked the design out of the park.

It was a little intimidating.

As they waited for Brandon to retrieve his head chef from the kitchen, Amara practiced her pitch over and over in her head. Even though he had been openly eager to work out some type of official arrangement, he told her he still needed to get approval from Alex—L.A. Cuchara's head chef and part owner.

"I'm sure Alex will love your desserts as much as I do,"

Brandon had told her over the phone. "But just in case, why don't you bring those peach *empanadas* you were telling me about the other day?"

Thankfully, the *empanadas* had turned out perfectly. The outside shells were golden brown, but still held the sheen of the sugared glaze she'd carefully brushed on each one. The fresh peach filling was both tart and sweet, with a subtle hint of cinnamon, nutmeg, and vanilla. Amara figured that if things went south with Alex then at least she and Daisy could drown their sorrows in butter and sugar on the drive back home.

She looked over at her cousin. Daisy had taken to biting her nails and bouncing her crossed legs, her gaze darting around the room like she expected a tiger to jump out from behind one of the restaurant's potted trees. "Hey, what's wrong with you?"

Daisy grabbed her shoulder. "*Mira*, Amara, I don't mean to be a downer, but dayum! This place is *muy* classy. Are you sure the *empanadas* are, you know, fancy enough?"

She'd been trying to push the same thought out of her head since they'd arrived. Maybe she should've made a crème brulee or a tiramisu, too.

But that's not you, Eric's voice whispered in her head.

The voice was right. How could she expect her parents or Brandon to believe in her desserts if she didn't? Amara decided it was time to start being her own fan girl. She turned to her cousin. "Well, if this Alex person doesn't think my *empanadas* are good enough for his restaurant then he can go straight to—"

"Amara..." Daisy tugged her shirt as she looked over Amara's shoulder. "Alex isn't a he. She's a she!"

"What?" She twisted in her chair just in time to see Brandon and a chesty brunette walking toward them. Although the brunette wore a black chef's coat, her ruby red lipstick and the white and red polka dot bandana tied around her hair reminded Amara of a 1940s pinup girl.

"She looks like a bitch," Daisy whispered.

"Stop. No, she doesn't," Amara whispered back.

"Look how close she's walking next to Brandon. She's marking her territory."

"You're being ridiculous. Knock it off. They're almost here." Amara stood up and glared at Daisy until she did the same.

Brandon and the brunette were all smiles when they finally reached the table.

"Amara! It's so good to see you again." He reached out both of his arms and she panicked. What if the brunette was more than his partner? What if she didn't like Amara hugging her man?

Too late. Brandon encased her with a strong embrace and a peck on the cheek. She didn't peck him back and instead tried to maneuver her way out of his arms as smoothly as possible.

"Good to see you too, Brandon." She smiled, stretching the corners of her mouth as far up her cheeks as they would go, to hide her nerves. "This is Daisy. She handles all of the bakery's marketing and special event catering."

She tried to telepathically warn Daisy to not say anything that would embarrass her. Luckily Brandon spoke before her cousin could. "So nice to meet you," he said, offering his hand. Amara let out a breath when Daisy shook it and only nodded back at him.

"Ladies, I'd like to introduce you to Alex, our head chef."

The brunette smiled warmly and Amara exhaled. She wasn't a bitch at all.

After everyone shook hands some more, Brandon motioned for them to sit down. "So Amara, I've been raving about you and your desserts to Alex for days now."

Her gut twisted in apprehension. "I hope my *empanadas* live up to the hype," she said, trying to laugh.

"Not to worry," the brunette said. "And, please, call me Alexa. Brandon here thinks he should've had a twin brother instead of a twin sister, so he's really the only one who ever calls me Alex."

"Twins?" Daisy finally opened her mouth. "Really?"

"Really. Once you spend some time with both of us, it's pretty easy to see the similarities. I'm the youngest," Alexa explained.

"Only by about four minutes," Brandon added. "Alex seems to think just because I came into this world 240 seconds before her, that that somehow makes me an old man."

"It does," Alexa said matter-of-factly. "That's why you're more responsible and I'm more fun."

Before Brandon could respond, Daisy chimed in. "Yep, you guys are definitely brother and sister. You sound just like Amara and her brother Miguel."

Everyone laughed and Amara silently thanked her cousin for lightening the mood. Time to talk business. "So, we know you both are very busy and we don't want to take up too much of your time. Would you like to try the dessert now?"

Alexa nodded and Brandon waved over the man who had been standing at another table folding linen napkins into the elaborate shapes that dotted tables all over the room. Within minutes, two other servers had brought over small plates, forks, and napkins and began pouring each of them a cup of coffee. Amara handed the box of pastries to another waiter who proceeded to serve the *empanadas*.

"These are traditional *empanada* desserts, except I've used a flourless dough and the filling is made with fresh peaches. I hope you enjoy."

"Mmmm," Daisy said with over-the-top enthusiasm that made Amara kick her in the shin. She went back to dissecting her own *empanada* with her fork and tried to sneak glances at the others. She could tell Brandon was enjoying his pastry by the appreciative sounds he made after every bite. Alexa was harder to read. Her chewing seemed slow and deliberate, yet the rest of her expression remained stoic.

Finally, Alexa set her fork down and picked up her napkin to wipe at the corners of her mouth.

"Well, Amara. I hate to admit when my brother is right, but this time I have no choice. These are incredible, and if everything else you bake is half as good, I would love to add your desserts to our menu."

"Woo hoo!" Daisy cheered.

Brandon beamed at Amara and reached across the table to grab her hand. "Welcome to the Cuchara restaurant family."

Two hours later she was still smiling. Her face hurt, but she didn't care. They'd stayed for *tapas*—Brandon's treat— and now they'd finally arrived back at the bakery.

While Daisy walked inside, Amara floated behind her. This was turning out to be one of the best nights of her life. She couldn't wait to tell Eric. He hadn't answered any of her phone calls and she didn't want to text him the news. It would be better to tell him in person so they could celebrate together like she'd promised.

"I still can't believe Alexa is Brandon's sister," she told her cousin after both dropped their purses onto the counter. "And you thought she was his girlfriend. Ha!"

"You know you thought it, too," Daisy insisted.

"Actually, I didn't. But, hey, this means he's available. You two had quite the conversation going on before we got in the car. I think he likes you," Amara said.

"Please. You two were the ones who wouldn't shut up. He barely even looked at me the entire time."

Was there a twinge of bitterness behind Daisy's words? Could it be that her cousin really had developed a little crush on their new business partner? After weeks of dealing with her incessant teasing about Eric, Amara jumped at the chance to turn the tables.

"Why, Daisy. Do I detect a little jealousy mixed in with your usual sarcasm tonight?"

"What are you talking about?"

"I think maybe you don't hate Brandon as much as you want me to think you do."

"Are you kidding me? Seriously?"

"Seriously."

"Okay, first of all, he's too arrogant and flashy for my taste. Second of all, if anyone is going to be jealous around here, it's going to be Eric once he realizes that Brandon is more interested in filling your *empanada* than your *empanada* filling—if you get my drift."

"What are you talking about?" They both jumped at his voice. Eric stood under the kitchen doorway. His arms folded. His mouth grim.

She shot an "I'll kill you later" look at Daisy before turning to face him. "It's nothing. Daisy is just trying to change the subject. I think she likes Brandon—"

"I heard that part. But what I want to know is who does Brandon like?"

"Well, I'm pooped," Daisy said with a fake yawn and stretch. "I'm going to head on home because I got something to do there and, yeah, I'm just going to go now. Goodnight!" And just like that, she was gone.

Coward.

"So is there something I should know about this Brandon guy? Did he decide he wants to take you out again?"

"What? No. Of course not. I told you, Daisy is just being Daisy. He's been nothing but professional with me. And good news! He wants to sell my desserts at L.A. Cuchara. Isn't that great?"

"It is, but now I'm wondering why. You have to admit, this whole thing is almost too good to be true. Maybe this Brandon guy is only giving you this opportunity because he wants to get in your pants?"

• • •

Even as he said the words he knew he didn't mean them. He regretted them even more when he saw the hurt and tears welling up in her eyes.

"You're an asshole," she blurted before spinning on her heels and heading toward the door.

Dammit!

He rushed after her, grabbed her wrist and pulled her against him. Wrapping his arms around her, he whispered apology after apology into her ear.

"You didn't deserve that. I'm so, so sorry. It's been a hell of a night and I shouldn't have taken it out on you."

"No, you shouldn't have," she said into his shoulder.

Of course he knew that Amara deserved this amazing opportunity. But the thought of Brandon being interested in her, or vice versa, had him seeing red. Especially when he was already hot under the collar thanks to an argument earlier with his mom.

He let go of her only to bring her face up toward his. Staring into her wet eyes, he pleaded one more time. "Can you forgive me?"

She nodded and he finally exhaled. Then he hugged her tight. They stood there for a couple of minutes, just holding onto each other. He could feel her heart beat against his chest, could hear her breathing.

If only they could stay like this. Forever.

Wait, what? Forever wasn't in the cards for him. Not with Amara.

She was the first to step back. "So are you ready to talk about it? What happened?"

Damn, she knew him so well. He didn't really want to talk about it, but after the shit he'd just thrown at her, she deserved better than a blow off. "Same old crap. I forgot to do something for my *abuela* and my mom went into one of her bitching sessions about how I can't do anything right."

"What did you forget to do?"

He scoffed. "Does it matter? It's like she looks for any excuse to remind me of all of the wrong things I've ever done in my life."

"I'm sorry. You can't let it get to you, though. Especially

when it comes to taking care of your *abuela*. It's been hard on you both. Maybe she just had a bad day and took it out on *you*. Sound familiar?"

He raised an eyebrow. "What are you trying to say?"

"All I'm saying is that maybe it's time for both of you to work out whatever it is between you two. And maybe you have to be the bigger person here and make the first move."

The bitterness that had been eating at him all night rumbled back to life. Even if he went with her suggestion, there was no way his mother would ever see him as the bigger person—no matter how hard he worked to take care of his *abuela,* or how much progress he made rebuilding his life. "Maybe I don't want to be the bigger person. Maybe I like being a jerk."

This time, her eyes showed both hurt and disappointment. What was wrong with him? Why was he ruining what was supposed to be a special night for them both?

She took a step away from him. "Well, I'm never going to be kind of girl who tells you it's okay to be a jerk, so maybe I should leave. We can do this another night."

He grabbed her face in both of his hands. "Hey, I'm just venting, that's all. I like that you call me out if I'm acting like a dick. It's good for me. *You're* good for me."

His whispered the last sentence against her lips and then kissed her, soft and gentle. But when she opened her mouth to him—all gentleness went out the window. Fighting the desire to rip her panties off and take her against the wall, Eric clung to his last ounce of self-control and tore his mouth away.

She protested and tried to pull his lips back down on hers.

"I know, sweetheart, I know," he said. "But I have a surprise for you."

He took her hand and led her through the blue plastic tarp hanging from the newly built wood-framed archway. It opened up into what had once been the bakery's catchall storage room. It was dark, except for small streams of light peeking through the seams of the brown butcher paper he'd taped across the front street window.

"Ta-da," he sang and flipped on the light switch.

"Oh, wow," she gasped. "You've done so much in here!"

Warmth spread across his chest as she acknowledged his work. He'd replaced the worn and cracked linoleum tiles with a dark, mahogany laminate wood floor. The dingy gray walls now radiated a warm golden yellow, and the room was nearly emptied of the assorted boxes and old fixtures that had been abandoned there over the years.

The only things left were part of his surprise. It took her a few seconds before she noticed.

In the far corner of the room, he'd set up a futon mattress and covered it with throw pillows and blankets. Two camping lanterns sat on either side of the mattress.

"And what's this?" She pulled him with her as she walked toward the makeshift bed.

"I know it's not a fancy hotel room, but…"

"It's perfect," she finished for him and put her arms around his neck.

He bent down and kissed her nose. "Hold that thought." Before she could protest, Eric reached down to turn on the lanterns. Then he ran back to the archway and turned off the lights. Amara waited where he left her, her body outlined in the fluorescent glow of the lanterns. She reached for him again, but he held up his index finger to let her know he had one more thing to do. He walked to the stepstool that held his iPod and pair of mini speakers.

Once he found the custom song list he created earlier, Eric hit play.

"Music, too? This is a full on seduction, isn't it?" Amara teased when he finally pulled her into his arms.

"Depends. Is it working?" he whispered in her ear.

"It's a good effort. But I think I might need a little more."

He loved that she'd become so playful when it came to sex. "Please share."

"Well, shouldn't there be some kissing? Like, for example, right here," she said as she pointed to her neck. He grinned even more and moved his lips right next to her finger. And before she could ask, he swirled his tongue in the same place.

"Ah…yes…this seduction is…starting off…very nicely," she murmured between his kisses and licks.

"You taste so good. So delicious," he murmured. His original plan to take it slow was quickly being revised in his head. He moved his hands to grab her ass and pull her tighter against his body, not sure if he could last one more minute without being inside her. The depths of his need should've frightened him. He hadn't needed anyone or anything like this in twelve years.

Except for alcohol.

Was that it? Had he simply replaced one addiction with another?

The feel of her soft lips on his distracted him from his self-interrogation. And when she moved her hands underneath his shirt and fanned them out across his stomach, pleasure rippled throughout his body. No, it wasn't an addiction. Sex with Amara had turned into more than just a quick fix or instant gratification. He'd needed alcohol to numb his pain, dull his senses. But this woman made him want to feel everything.

She was running through his veins now. He'd come back to life without even realizing it. Because of her. Only her.

He groaned and took her mouth, easing her down onto the mattress, their legs twisting together as he ground his bulging erection against her pussy over and over again. The friction was driving him beyond crazy and he decided the seduction was over. He moved one hand under her skirt and slid it along her inner thigh until he reached the vee between her legs.

"Yes," she gasped.

"Yes, what?"

"Touch me. Please."

He pulled her panties to the side and slid his index finger between her folds. He groaned. Hot. So hot. For *him*. Her legs opened to give him better access to her sex and he rewarded her by thrusting another finger inside.

"Oh my God! I'm going to come!" Her moans echoed throughout the empty, small room. It gave him such fucking satisfaction to know that he was responsible for her cries of pleasure. It also made him crazy horny. He couldn't wait any longer and pulled his fingers out so he could focus on rubbing her clit with long, hard strokes. Seconds later, he claimed her mouth as she shrieked to high heaven as an orgasm rocked her body.

"Take off your jeans," she said against his lips.

It sent a thrill straight to his groin. "Whatever you want."

Eric kissed her one last time and then stood up to take off his clothes. Amara wiggled out of hers and he joined her naked body back on the mattress.

He looked at her, taking in the perfectness of the moment. All of the anger and frustration he felt earlier had completely disappeared.

She did that.

He moved down her body and opened her up for him. The foil packet was already in place next to the mattress, and it took him only seconds to rip it open and slide on the condom. Positioning himself in between her legs, he grabbed his sheathed cock and rubbed it against the glistening lips of her pussy. He loved that she was always so wet for him.

"Are you ready for me, sweetheart?" Her flushed cheeks and taut nipples screamed that she was. But he needed to hear the words.

"I want you," she moaned.

Those three little words filled him up in ways he couldn't explain with words. They unraveled him, yet also completed him all at the same time. In that moment, there was no other man who could give Amara what she craved.

Savor it. Cherish it for as long as she'll let you.

Problem was, he wasn't so sure he could accept anything short of forever now that she'd gotten to him. *Inside* him. He leaned down and kissed her deep and hard. Looking into her eyes, he growled, "Tell me you're mine."

"I'm yours," she said between gasps.

"Tell me I'm the only one you want inside you."

"You're the only one I want inside me."

And with one deep thrust, he gave them both what they needed.

Chapter Twelve

"Didn't you get embarrassed, you know, having a good-looking stranger looking at your...you know," Amara asked.

"My vajayjay?" Trina answered. "Oh, trust me. There was some embarrassment. But as soon as a contraction hit, I got over that and wanted him as far in there as he could get if it meant getting the baby out quicker."

"Trina!" Amara's mother huffed. "You're a mother now and mothers don't speak of such things."

Only Amara could see Trina's eye roll. She stifled a laugh and got back to attempting to fold the smallest pair of footed pajamas she'd ever seen. The three of them were sitting in Miguel and Trina's living room folding laundry together, but she kept getting distracted by the overall cuteness of every single piece of clothing and the adorable baby smell they exuded. Her mother's pile of folded clothes was much taller than Amara's or Trina's— a fact that was not lost on her mother and her mother's evil eye.

"Sorry, Consuelo," Trina said. "I've only had about two hours of sleep in the last two days. I'm a little out of it."

Amara's mother heaved a long, exaggerated sigh. "I tell you to sleep when he sleeps. Why don't you go in the bedroom and lie down for a while?"

"That's okay. I want to stay out here and catch up with Amara." Trina turned her body toward her and gave her the knowing look that said she needed some saving from Consuelo's helpful "advice."

"So Amara, what's going on with you? Anything new and interesting?"

"Nothing really." *Oh, except for the fact I'm having the best sex of my life with Eric, and I landed a huge contract for the bakery.*

Even if her mother hadn't been sitting there, Amara still wouldn't have told Trina about either one. She loved her sister-in-law but she'd been known to blab to Miguel, who then would blab to her parents. She couldn't risk it, so she kept quiet.

"Come on," Trina begged. "Give me some gossip and good old fashioned girl talk. I need some grownup time… please."

"Well, I did hear that they were going to finally close down that bar on Soto Street. There was another fight there last weekend and I heard the owner has had enough dealing with all the winos that hang out on Thursday nights."

Trina sighed almost as loudly as Consuelo had. "That's not gossip. It was in the newspaper this morning. I meant tell me something juicy, something not everyone knows yet."

She shrugged. "I got nothing." Well, besides her own racy secret, but she wasn't about to divulge that no matter how bored her sister-in-law was.

"You're no fun. Fine. Let's talk about Eric, then."

Amara focused on snapping the tiny buttons on a new pair of pajamas she'd grabbed from the laundry basket. She didn't dare look at Trina—or her mother. "Wha...what do you mean?"

"I mean tell me how he's doing with the remodel? What has it been like with him working there?"

"How would Amara know? He only comes to the bakery at night." Consuelo answered for her before standing up and heading toward the back of the house. "I'll go check to see if the other load of blankets is ready."

Though she usually hated when her mother answered for her, this time Amara was grateful. She didn't trust the sound of her voice at that moment.

"Hmm, well I was just wondering how much progress he's made," Trina continued. "I was telling Miguel that I was surprised he wasn't supervising him more. What happens if he relapses and goes on some type of a bender? You know it's a challenge every day for recovering alcoholics to stay sober."

Amara stopped pretending to fold. "Eric is an alcoholic?"

"Oh. Dammit! I wasn't supposed to say anything," Trina cringed. "Don't say anything to Miguel, okay?"

Why didn't he tell her? Sure, alcoholism wasn't exactly an appropriate topic for late night pillow talk, but if he told Miguel why wouldn't he tell her, too?

Because you're not his girlfriend and you never wanted to be, remember?

"Amara, hello? Did you hear me?" Trina's voice interrupted her thoughts.

"Yes, I heard you. Of course, I won't tell Eric or Miguel that I know. I mean if it was important for me to know then he would've told me himself."

She had been referring to Eric, but Trina thought she was talking about Miguel.

"Well, Eric asked him not tell anyone. He didn't want people judging him even more, I guess. Don't get me wrong, I'm not judging him either. I just think Miguel needs to be less trusting. After all, we don't really know this guy anymore."

Amara wondered if she'd ever get to know him. "So, does he seem different to you?"

Trina shrugged. "It's hard to tell. He came over to watch a game one night before the baby was born and that was the first time I'd actually talked to him since he got back. He was more quiet than I remember. I told Miguel that and he laughed and said Eric probably just needed to get laid."

Amara choked on the water she'd just drank.

"Oh, sorry," Trina said in hushed tones. "Maybe I shouldn't have told you that either. Geez, I blame these bullshit postpartum hormones. It's like fucking truth serum."

"It's fine, Trina. I'm fine. Go on."

"Well, that's pretty much it. Miguel actually tried to set him up on a blind date with one of our friends who's not really our friend. It's this big, old, long story that I'll bore you with another time. Anyway, I was against it but Miguel insisted."

Her mouth went dry. She had to take another drink of her water before talking again. "So what happened?"

Trina handed her another basket of clothes. "Nothing. Eric turned him down."

She tried not to smile. "Did he say why?"

"Yeah, he said he didn't come back here to find a girl-friend. He just wants to focus on doing a good job for your dad so that he can use him as a reference to get more jobs down the line."

Her mother walked back into the room and both of them knew it was time to change the subject. But as the conversation turned toward baby this and baby that, Amara's thoughts drifted again.

Why did it bother her so much that he hadn't told her about his drinking? She'd been clear since that first night that their arrangement was temporary. He didn't owe her anything. Especially, not explanations about the past twelve years.

Trina was right. They really didn't know Eric anymore. It was almost like she'd been sleeping with a complete stranger—something she would have never done before. In fact, she was doing a lot of things she never expected to do. She thought that had been a good thing, but now she wasn't so sure.

Still, part of her wanted to know what he'd been through.

And the other part wanted to know why she cared so much.

• • •

Eric had been in trouble enough times in his life to know he was in it now. Only difference was, for once, he had no idea why.

All he knew is that when he showed up to the bakery that afternoon, Amara started acting weird. He couldn't tell if she was mad or sad. Even as he helped her carefully pack the desserts she was going to show her parents as part of her plan to partner with L.A. Cuchara, he couldn't decide whether she looked as though she was about to cry, or rip into him about something.

"These look great, Amara," he offered, hoping to get some type of conversation going.

"I don't know. This one looks a little too brown." She pointed to a perfectly golden *empanada* inside the pink bakery box.

"Really? I think it looks like all the others."

"Who's the baker here? We're not talking paint samples. You may know the difference between eggshell white and classic white, but I think I know what I'm talking about when it comes to pastries. And this *empanada* is burned."

She pulled the flaky dessert out of the box and walked over to the trashcan.

He looked at Daisy for some explanation, but she only shrugged and headed into the kitchen. It was up to him to find out what was wrong with Amara.

After tossing the lone *empanada* in the trash, she came back to the counter and studied the half-filled box.

"Hey," he said finally. "What's going on with you today? I totally get that this is a big deal for you, but sweetheart, you're kind of acting a little crazy." He winced when he said the last part—a reaction he'd learned early on, whenever he told the woman in his life that they needed to calm the fuck down. At least he didn't use those exact words with Amara.

But unlike those other women, she didn't yell or slap him across the face.

"It's nothing," she said instead. She didn't even look at

him.

He knew her well enough to know she was lying.

"I know it's not nothing. Please, just tell me." He reached out to touch her hand but she snapped it away and headed into the kitchen.

"We'll talk later," she said over her shoulder.

He knew he should leave it at that for the moment. The old Eric wouldn't have cared, wouldn't have wasted another second worrying about what some girl felt or needed. But that was the problem right there, he realized. Amara wasn't just "some girl," and he wasn't the old Eric anymore. He gritted his teeth and stalked into the kitchen after her. "I think we need to talk *now*."

Daisy raised her eyebrows and muttered something about cleaning windows then walked out, leaving them alone to face each other from opposite sides of the kitchen.

Amara twirled an errant strand from her ponytail and shifted her weight from one foot to the other. "Can't we forget it about it? Please?"

"I don't know what we're supposed to be forgetting. You haven't told me a thing, remember? But somehow I've managed to piss you off, and I think I deserve to know what the hell I did!"

She flinched at his hard tone, but then her eyes went cold. "Fine. I'm upset because you never told me what happened to you!"

It was his turn to flinch. He'd never heard Amara yell at anyone. She was right, though. Here he'd been thinking they were on the verge of this thing between them turning into more than a "thing," and yet, he hadn't trusted her with his past. His secrets.

It made him feel like an ass.

Determined to make things right, he crossed the room and tried to pull her into his arms, but she stood motionless. He sighed and settled for holding her stiff body against his.

"I know we're not in a real relationship," she said, "but you know everything about me and what I'm going through, and there are twelve years of your life that are a complete mystery to me." She softened and pressed her forehead to his shoulder. "I'm not saying you have to tell me all your secrets because I could care less if you're on the lam, or some secret government spy. It's just hard to trust you with my future when I don't even know your past."

My future. God, he loved hearing the words, even if he'd yet to earn them. He let go of her so he could look into her eyes. "Ask me anything. I promise to tell you whatever you want to know."

She looked unconvinced. "Really? Anything?"

Nodding, he took her hand and was relieved when she clasped his fingers. And she didn't let them go for the next twenty minutes. He told her how devastated he'd felt when Mariah miscarried, but how it was nothing compared to when she'd confirmed his suspicion that the baby wasn't even his, and that she'd only let him believe it was because the other guy wouldn't have wanted her to keep it.

He'd dodged a bullet, for sure. And although he'd felt some relief, he also felt anger. Lots of it. So he started drinking that night and didn't stop. Not until he totally missed his graduation ceremony and woke up in his car a day later in some parking lot in Montebello. When he got home his mom was hysterical, telling him how he'd devastated his *abuela*. He still felt the sting of her words: the one thing she wanted more than anything in this world was to see her only grandson get his high school diploma and he couldn't even give that to her. It didn't matter that the ceremony was just for show, that he could still go pick up his diploma. His mom kicked him out then and there—just five days before his eighteenth birthday.

"So where'd you go?" she asked. "Why didn't you come to our house?"

"I guess I was ashamed. I didn't want to pull you or your family into my drama. So I slept in my car for a few nights and then I called one of my cousins who lived in Las Vegas. He said I could crash there and that's where I've been all this time."

"And the drinking?"

He winced at the question. "When you've been doing it since you were fourteen, every day is a fight to stay sober. But it's under control. I have a sponsor, and I found a good AA meeting here. I've only been a couple of times but it's a good group and it helps me, knowing they're there when I need them."

"I'm glad you're still going to meetings. You don't ever need to be ashamed to ask for help. And that includes asking me."

"It's not that I'm ashamed. Well, maybe it is a little. But part of it is I don't want to drag you into my problems. You've got your hands full here, and the last thing you need is to worry about whether I'm sneaking shots of whiskey while I'm installing your drywall."

He laughed to hide his own anxiousness. It was true. He needed Amara's trust, and telling her all of his failures and weaknesses wasn't exactly the best way to earn it.

"I won't think that," she said, and he believed her. "All I ask is that you're honest with me. I can't sleep with someone I don't trust."

He moved his hands back to her waist and pulled her against him. Her eyes widened and he smiled. "So that means you're still willing to sleep with me?"

She pulled his head down for a kiss. His heart quickened at the taste of her—delicious and sweet and sexy all at once.

"What do you think?" she asked, teasing him with her words and soft lips.

The warmth of her body and the feel of her breasts against his chest stirred his cock, and he groaned as he felt it straining against his jeans. Eric couldn't hold back any longer. He grabbed her by the ass and lifted her up onto the stainless steel counter. He moved his hands to her head and kissed her deep, their tempo and passion building.

"Damn, I want to fuck you right here," he murmured against her lips as his hands cupped the sides of her breasts through her thin T-shirt.

"Keep doing that and I might just let you," she said in a breath. He believed her and that made him nearly explode in his jeans.

"But I can't. Right?" He knew they couldn't have sex in the bakery's kitchen. Daisy could walk in any minute, so could a customer. Hell, so could her parents. He still needed to double check though. Because if she said okay, he'd be inside her within a matter of seconds.

"Right. We can't," she answered back. "Tonight, though. Tonight for sure. Okay?"

He nodded, knowing that if they didn't stop soon, he wouldn't be able to control his body any longer. So he tore his lips away and dropped his head onto her shoulder. His ragged breathing eventually slowed. His heartbeat went back to normal. His jeans became more comfortable. And when he trusted himself to touch her with his hands again, he picked her up and set her gently back onto the floor.

Jingle. Jingle.

They looked at each other and smiled at having stopped just in time.

"Tonight, then?" He searched her eyes for any lingering doubt about him or his intentions. Maybe it was his simmering desire or his own naive hope, but he didn't see any.

"Tonight," she assured him.

As he left the bakery, he tried not to think about how few "tonights" they had left.

Chapter Thirteen

The night didn't end up going *quite* the way Eric envisioned, though he wasn't complaining.

Amara had come back to the bakery at nine o'clock, but she'd stumbled in loaded down with presentation folders, sticky notes, poster board, markers, glue sticks, and different stacks of paper.

He hurried over to help before she tripped and fell. "Do you have homework or something?" he joked.

"Actually, *we* have homework. I've been going over everything I'm going to say to my parents tomorrow, and the one thing that kept nagging at me was how unprofessional it'll look. The last thing I need is for them to think this isn't a real business meeting. In their minds, it'll probably just be another morning at the bakery, talking to Amara about her crazy ideas. So I think I came up with a way to make them take me more seriously."

"With all of this stuff?"

"Exactly. I'm going to do a real, professional business presentation, complete with handouts, charts, and diagrams. I started some of it already but I can't do this by myself." She looked at him, her eyes a little too wide. "So what do you think? Am I being stupid? Maybe this was all a bad idea."

In all his life, he'd never seen someone so determined to make her dream come true, yet still so afraid. He'd promised to help her, so if that meant spending the rest of the night coloring pie charts or cutting out pictures instead of rocking her world, so be it. "I think that maybe I would've done a lot more homework back in high school if you had been there helping me," he said. "Amara, I know you can do this. Let's get to work."

She threw her arms around him. Planting quick kisses on his forehead and cheeks, she thanked him over and over again.

The contact immediately made him grow hard. So much for keeping himself under control for a few more hours. "I'm sorry, sweetheart, but those cute little pecks aren't going to cut it. I need to *taste* you."

He claimed her lips, and the way she immediately opened to him threw gasoline on his already burning desire for her. He hauled her body against him, and she groaned or sighed or hummed, he wasn't sure. What he *was* sure of was that the vibration against his lips drove him crazy—so crazy that he worried he'd never be sane again. So he deepened the kiss and moved his hand between her legs. Although the crinkly, thin fabric of her long skirt created a barrier, he could still feel the heat of her pussy underneath. He took satisfaction in knowing that he'd made her so hot, and the more he rubbed, the hotter—and wetter—she got.

He moved his lips to her neck and then to the top of her shirt, pushing the edge of it down with his chin as he went.

"God, I want to bend you over and fuck you right here," he growled.

"Then do it. Our homework can wait."

It was all he needed to hear. He guided her into the back storage room and locked the door. It didn't matter that it was late; they'd left the front lights on and he couldn't risk her dad or brother walking in and seeing what he was about to do to her.

Eric moved his hand behind Amara's head and took her mouth again. His tongue swept the bottom of her lip and she nipped it, sending a cascade of shocks through his body. He loved it and would gladly let her bite him all night.

But his dick had other plans.

He reached between them and found the hem of her shirt and pulled it over her head, unveiling a lacy purple bra that was so sexy he decided to leave it on. Then his hands slid down the sides of her body, pulling her skirt and panties with them until they reached her ankles. He lifted each foot gently, opening her thighs as he went, then knelt in front of her.

"Sweetheart, I need you to grab hold of my workbench behind you and hang on."

Before she could ask why, he spread the glistening lips of her pussy and took a long, deep lick.

"Ohhhhh," she gasped and arched her back, her thighs quivering as they made contact with the stubble of his jawline.

"Fuck, yeah," he whispered back, lost in his own reckless lust and need. Although he loved tasting her sweetness, he knew the world wouldn't be right again until he could slide his cock in where his tongue was now.

He took one last suck and then stood up. "Turn around and bend over," he ordered.

As she did, he worked furiously to undo his belt and scramble out of his jeans. Within seconds, he'd removed his boxer briefs and sheathed his cock.

He focused on the glorious sight before him. Amara was bent over his workbench with her ass in the air. He couldn't resist planting a kiss on each cheek, his finger trailing from her clit to the dimples at the base of her back.

"God, you have a beautiful ass," he said. "I'm going to enjoy grabbing hold of it while I pound into your pussy."

With one hard thrust, he was inside her, and as promised, he held on tight, digging into the flesh of her ass as he pulled her against him over and over again.

"Do you like me fucking you this way, baby?"

"Yes. Oh. Yes. Oh," she answered between thrusts.

"I knew you would. You know why?"

"Why?"

"Because deep down you're a naughty, naughty girl who loves her pussy licked and loves to be fucked from behind with your ass in the air. Tell me that you're a naughty girl, Amara."

"I'm a...I'm a naughty girl," she cried out.

Her words and the clenching muscles of her pussy around his cock unraveled his control. He leaned across her back and hooked one arm under her so he could drive in deeper. Her body shook as the orgasm rolled through her and it set off his own physical and emotional eruption.

And in the aftermath, he knew he was well and truly

screwed.

. . .

Why does it feel like I'm going to a job interview?

Nerves jumbled her insides, so much so that she could barely force down a cup of coffee earlier. Now, as she stood staring at the front door, waiting, she didn't just feel nauseated, she felt faint.

Daisy, on the other hand, was happily munching on a doughnut. "Hey, why do you look so pale? It's just your parents," she said with a wink.

Amara glared at her cousin.

They were about to present their ideas to Ricardo and Consuelo on how they planned to revamp the bakery. Despite her mother's wishes, she'd actually convinced Señora Rios to change her order back to the fondant cake by telling her how unique and special it would be. The cake had been such a hit with her grandson that Señora Rios asked Daisy and Amara to take care of her anniversary party next month.

The business was already growing and they hadn't changed much. Now it was up to her to make her parents see just how much more could be done.

"Okay, we're here," her mother announced as she opened the bakery's front door. "Let's get this done quickly. I have to go help the ladies at the church get ready for the rummage sale next weekend." Her dad entered after her and Amara directed them to have a seat at the table.

Her hands shook as she gathered the presentation folders she and Eric had created last night after having sex…

twice. Each contained a proposed gourmet selection of new desserts and coffees all targeted to bring in the students and faculty of neighboring Cal State Los Angeles. Amara had also included a list of the traditional breads and desserts they would keep on the menu because they were still popular sellers, and a note that she would continue taking cake and cupcake orders for the weekends—with a few new options for cake flavors and fillings.

Daisy's contribution included screen captures of a new website, Facebook page, and Twitter account—things they knew her parents wouldn't quite understand at first but were necessary to show their strategy to attract the college customers. She also listed local events where Amara could sell desserts, a draft of advertising fliers, and a mock-up of a new bakery logo: a white line drawing of a steaming cup of coffee next to a piece of bread inside a brown square.

Eric's section showed hand-drawn diagrams of a new floor layout that included a new public restroom area and opened up the entire front space of the bakery with new slimmer display cases that Eric would build on his own. He'd added swatches of deep oranges and yellows – his suggestions for repainting the building's exterior. Finally, he'd drawn a few more tables for the inside and outside to encourage people to stay at the bakery while they ate pastries and drank coffee.

The last section of the presentation folder included a trial business agreement with L.A. Cuchara for the restaurant to exclusively sell Robles' gourmet desserts for the next three months as part of a special weekend menu. Amara would bake the desserts at a negotiated discounted price, and in return, Brandon would help promote the bakery with signage and fliers inside the restaurant.

"Well, what do you think?" Amara asked after going through the presentation page by page with her parents.

"How much?" Her dad was the first to speak. "How much is all of this going to cost me?"

"Nothing," Amara said.

"Don't be ridiculous! More chairs and tables, new display counters. Expanding the space! This is all going to cost money, Amara," her mother interjected.

"Mom, can you let me finish, please? Anything that is in addition to what you originally hired Eric for is not going to cost you and dad a thing, because I'm going to pay for it."

Consuelo's eyes grew big. "With what? You have no money."

"I'm going to get a small business loan."

"Again, with what? You have no collateral. No bank is going to give you money without you putting something up for it."

"That's why I want you to sign the bakery over to me."

"*Estás loca!*" her mother said with a laugh. "After what happened last time? No, Amara. No."

The words stung. Maybe her mother was right. Maybe she was crazy. After all, she'd tried once before and failed on an epic scale. Part of her wanted to tell her parents never mind, to just forget the plan. But she heard Eric's voice urging her to stand up to them to tell them once and for all what she wanted.

She lifted her chin and pressed on. "I know how hard it'll be to trust me with the bakery. But things are different now. I know what it's going to take to make this a successful business. But to do it, I need to be the one in charge. This bakery is going to close if you don't let me save it."

"We don't need you to save it," her dad insisted.

"Stop, Daddy, just stop. We both know you're having a hard time making the payments on the loan you took out on the house. I work here every day. I know how much money we're making—or rather how much money we're *not* making."

"It's not that bad," her mom said with a sniff.

"I'm sorry. But it is."

Her dad shot up from his chair, his face red and contorted. "We've been through tough times before and we always survived. This is my business and I'll fix it."

"But Dad—"

"But nothing. I'm sorry, *mija*. I know you're only trying to help, but taking the bakery away from us isn't the way to do it. I'll find another way."

Amara looked at her mother, expecting her to tell her again why this had all been a crazy idea.

Instead, her eyes were sad. Her face? Scared. And that's when Amara realized that her mother knew just how bad the situation was now, and how bad it was going to get if something didn't change soon.

And that broke her heart even more.

Chapter Fourteen

Eric propped the sheet of drywall against the new granite countertop he'd already covered with a tarp. He looked around and checked off the list of prep steps in his head. Everything was ready and in place to replace the drywall in the bakery's kitchen. Now he just needed Miguel to show up so he could get started.

He checked his watch again. Fifteen minutes past six. The bakery had been closed for more than an hour and he still hadn't done a thing.

Where was Miguel, and why hadn't he called?

Apparently none of the Robles siblings knew how to use a phone today.

He'd been waiting for a call or a text from Amara since that afternoon to let him know how the meeting with her parents went. No news didn't necessarily mean good news. At first he was worried, but then as the minutes grew into hours, he became irritated. He knew it was silly to expect that he'd be the first on her list to call either way it went. But didn't he at least rate in the top five?

Maybe the news was good, and she and her family were out celebrating right now?

Eric stomped over to his tool bag and pulled out his phone. A black screen met his glare. He pushed buttons, but nothing happened. Nothing was going to happen. His phone had died and he'd left his charger back at the house.

Son of a bitch.

His anger diminished slightly. Perhaps Amara or Miguel had tried to call him after all. He shoved his phone into his back pocket and looked around for a paper and something to write with. It would only take him about ten minutes to run home and come back, but he didn't want to chance Miguel showing up and thinking he was the one who had bailed.

Eric walked to the front of the bakery in search of something he could write a note on, but before he got to the cash register, he heard a key turning the lock on the front door.

Instead of Miguel appearing on the other side, Amara poked her head in and met his eyes.

"What are you doing here?" He didn't mean to blurt it out but she'd surprised him.

"I came to find out why you're not answering your phone or the bakery's phone. Miguel says he's been trying to call you for the past forty-five minutes."

"Oh. Yeah, sorry. I just realized my cell is dead. I was going to run to the house and get my charger."

"What about the bakery's phone? Miguel says it just rings and rings and rings."

"I unplugged it. We were going to be working on the kitchen walls tonight and the wires from the phone in there were in the way."

She walked inside and he pulled her against him for a kiss. All of the frustration he'd felt earlier melted away in her arms. He noticed, though, that something was off about her. He ended the kiss and asked the question he had a feeling he already knew the answer to. "How did it go with your parents?"

"Not good, of course. You can still work on the remodel, though, so at least I didn't screw that up." She wrapped her arms around herself, and his chest ached at how defeated she looked. "Anyway, I didn't come over here to talk about them. I came to tell you that Miguel can't make it tonight after all. Something happened on a job site today and he had to drive all the way to San Diego. He thought he'd be back in time but his boss is making him stay overnight. He says he won't be able to come help you until Friday after work."

He wanted to press her for details about her parents, but now he had another problem. "Friday? Well, that kind of sucks."

"Why? What's the problem?

"He was going to hold the drywall sheets in place while I screwed them into the studs. I usually rent a lift if I'm going to do it by myself. Guess now I have to wait to do it until Friday. That means I'll be behind schedule a few days."

"Sorry, Eric," she said, and reached out to touch his shoulder

"It's fine, really. I'll just work Saturday night and all day Sunday to catch up."

"But that would mean you'd be working for twenty-four

hours straight."

He shrugged. "I've done it before. Besides I have no other choice. I don't want to cost you guys any extra money if I fall behind."

"Then you do have a choice after all. I can stay and help you."

"Help me hang the drywall? No way."

"Why not?"

"Because you don't know how."

"You said you just need someone to hold it up for you, right? I think I'm perfectly capable of doing that."

"Thanks for the offer, but I don't think I could handle seeing you handle my power tools, And, beautiful, you'd be too much of a distraction. Besides, don't you have to be back here again at four in the morning?"

"As long as I get to sleep by eleven, I'll be fine. That gives us about four hours. Will that be enough time?"

"I don't know, Amara. I don't think your parents would like it very much if they found out you were helping me."

"Why? Miguel helps you all the time. What's the difference?"

"Uh, I think we both know the difference."

"I'm a big girl. I can go out at night by myself. As long as I tell them I'm staying out and I have my keys, they'll go to bed and not think twice about me."

"Are you sure?"

"Positive. Let me call my mom first and then we can get started."

For the next three hours, Amara and Eric worked side by side installing sheets of drywall. He'd even let her screw in a couple of the sheets herself. They didn't do much chitchatting, since they were focused on getting the project done before Amara had to leave, and it was obvious to him that the meeting with her parents still weighed heavily on her mind.

Because she'd been so quiet, he hadn't been as distracted as he thought he'd be.

Fine. He'd been distracted a few times. Like when he got a closeup view of her ass as she climbed up his ladder.

"Are you sure I'm doing it right?" she called down to him. "Wait. Were you staring at my butt just now?"

He jerked his head in the opposite direction. "No. Of course not."

"Of course you weren't." He could hear the smile behind her words and he grinned, too. The mood instantly lightened between them.

When she finished, he held the ladder for her as she made her way back down toward solid ground. But she stopped at the last rung, which made her just a few inches taller than him.

"It's a good thing that you weren't staring at my butt earlier."

"And why is that?"

"Because I'm not going to stare at yours while you pack up all this stuff."

He laughed and grabbed her off the ladder, then spun her around once and set her down to give her a quick kiss. They worked together to fold up the tarps. As she focused intently on making sure the corner of each tarp folded over onto each other exactly, he couldn't help but notice how nice it had been to have her there. And they hadn't even had sex.

He'd never met anyone so generous, so selfless, so

beautiful on the inside and out. She'd stayed to help him even though hanging drywall was the probably the last thing she'd wanted to do after dealing with her parents. Still, she'd pushed through without complaining once. She was definitely a trooper, and he hated to see her so deflated. He wanted to make it all better. But how?

He took the folded tarp from her then grabbed her hand. "So, are you ready to talk about what happened with your parents? Is everything okay?"

She nodded, but he could see the weariness behind it. The urge to take her into his arms and soothe her worries revved up inside him. "It's fine," she said, and sighed. "I should've known they'd never go for it."

"Tell me what happened."

"What always happens. They don't trust me with the bakery because of that stupid cupcake shop fiasco. I get it, I do. But at some point they're going to have realize that I'm their only hope, right? Or maybe I just need to accept the fact that it's never going to happen and eventually the bakery will close and I'll have to get a job decorating cakes at the supermarket."

"Don't think like that. You can't give up, not yet."

"Then when? I'm serious, Eric. Sometimes I wonder why I even bother trying for something that I know is such a long shot."

Her sense of defeat pained him. He was usually the negative one, not her. There had to be a way for him to show her that all was not lost.

"Stop being so hard on yourself," he said, and pulled her into his arms. "You convinced them to let me finish the remodel, and that's huge."

She nodded with a tired smile. "Honestly, it was more Miguel than me. I guess you two are back to being friends?"

"Yeah, things are cool." *But only because he doesn't know about us.*

"Good, I'm glad," she said with a yawn. "Okay, I guess I'm more tired than I thought."

"Yeah, it's getting late. You should go home and get to bed." Although he hated to, he released her.

But she didn't move. He smiled at her, but stopped when he realized she wasn't smiling back. Instead, her brow furrowed and she bit her lip. She looked serious, determined even. His heart beat faster, and he swallowed hard as he waited for her to say whatever was on her mind.

"Despite being disappointed about everything else, I am glad you're going to be sticking around for awhile. I know we're trying to keep things, um, casual between us, so is that okay that I said that?"

It was only a whisper, yet it reverberated through his whole body. The invisible chains that had kept him from letting her know what she did to him or what she was beginning to mean to him fell down around his ankles. He couldn't lie to her now if he tried.

"I don't know," he whispered back. "Is it okay for me to say I'm glad that I get to be around you some more, too?"

The slow smile on her face stopped his heart. "Yes, that's definitely okay. That's great, even."

He could tell she meant the words, and that surprised him. But before he could say anything else, she turned and walked out of the bakery, her hips swaying back and forth like a pendulum, hypnotizing him, so he couldn't even think of going after her. Because if he'd caught her, he'd want to lay more than just drywall.

And it wasn't until much later that he realized that swaying had been deliberate, even exaggerated.

His laugh bellowed throughout the empty bakery.

Amara Robles had made damn sure he'd watch her ass as she left.

Chapter Fifteen

There was nothing more depressing than a rainy day in Los Angeles.

Especially when the gray, gloomy skies matched your already miserable mood.

Amara attempted a smile when thanking the man who bought three dollars worth of *pan dulce,* but stopped trying when he grumbled back some unintelligible response.

Yep, the rain made everyone a sour puss.

Her stomach rumbled and reminded her it was time for lunch. She thought about texting Daisy to bring her a sandwich when she came in later, but decided against it. It was too cold for a sandwich. She was too sad for a sandwich. What she needed was something warm and full of carbs and calories. She needed comfort food.

Amara looked around the bakery. There were definitely carbs and calories galore, yet, nothing she'd made sounded good. Her eyes roamed the shop one more time until they stayed on the container filled with rolls.

Capirotada.

Her mouth salivated just at the thought of her homemade Mexican bread pudding. She did a quick mental inventory of the pantry and thanked God that she had what she needed to make one special batch just for herself.

Two hours later, it was ready.

This time her smile came naturally. Amara looked down at the first piece she'd just served herself and noted that although it looked like a jumbled mess, it smelled intoxicating. It was a sweet, spicy aroma that screamed holidays with family, cozy evenings by the fireplace and all the things that had ever made her feel warm and happy. She cut into the dessert with her fork and took a bite. Melted, salty butter and cheddar cheese mingled with a sweet syrup made from *piloncillo*, cinnamon, and cloves. The mixture coated raisins, pecans, and warm, mushy pieces of day-old *bolillo* rolls. *Capirotada* had always reminded her of a rustic French toast casserole, but the addition of the dried fruit and other components made it more like a bread pudding. It was both sweet and savory, decadent and nourishing.

It was the perfect comfort food.

She took another bite just as Daisy walked through the front door. Her cousin stopped, turned up her nose, and took a deep whiff.

"Do I smell *capirotada*?" she asked, looking around.

"Maybe," Amara answered with her mouth still full.

Daisy walked over to her and spotted the small casserole dish on the counter. She raised her eyebrows. "But it's not Friday. I thought you only made *capirotada* on Fridays so you could use the stale rolls that didn't sell during the week?"

"I needed it. It's been a helluva week."

"It's only Wednesday."

Amara popped another piece into her mouth. "Exactly."

"Hey," Daisy said. "Don't eat all of it. I want some, too."

Her cousin helped herself to a serving and moaned around her first mouthful. "Oh. My. God. It's still warm, and the cheese is all gooey. I always think the cheese doesn't belong when I watch you make it, but then I take a bite and it's perfect."

"It's really no different from adding fruit to cottage cheese—the sweet goes with the salty," Amara explained, and dug in for another bite. "You know some people actually make apple pies with cheddar cheese, too? It looks and sounds off, but it works."

The two of them polished off half of the casserole dish. "Our *abuela* was the one who taught me how to make *capirotada*," Amara said. "Every now and then, I think of ways to tweak the recipe, make it more sophisticated, but I never end up doing it because this is one of those foods that's more about tradition than style. When I make it like she used to, I feel close to her. It makes me happy, no matter what's going on in my life at the time."

Daisy nodded. "Ah. So this was a I'm-depressed-because-my-parents-shot-down-my-bakery-ideas-again *capirotada*?"

"You could say that."

Her cousin gave her a side hug. "I'm sorry, Amara. I wish I could've said something or done something to change their mind."

"I know you do. But I don't think there's anything—"

Amara stopped mid-sentence as her dad opened the bakery's front door, looking stiff and uncomfortable. He walked over to the counter and nodded once.

Although it wasn't unusual for him to stop by, she hadn't been prepared for the stomach flop his unexpected visit caused. She hoped he didn't want to talk again about what happened. No matter how happy her *abuela's capirotada* made her, she wasn't sure it would be enough.

"Hey Dad, what's going on? Did you need something?"

"Well, not really. I just needed to talk to you about something."

"I'll go find something to do in the kitchen," Daisy said, and started to back away.

"No, Daisy. You stay. This affects you, too."

Amara's stomach flopped again, then flipped. Now what?

Her dad cleared his throat and braced himself on the counter with both hands. "Your mother and I have changed our minds about the bakery."

Her mouth dropped open. "Really?" Hope welled inside her heart, but she knew to push it down until she heard everything he had to say first.

"We decided we are going to let you go ahead with your plans for the remodel and new menu, but we're still not selling the bakery to you."

"Then how are you going to pay for everything?"

"I spoke to Mr. Montoya and we signed an agreement today. His first deposit should cover the costs of the rest of the remodel and some of the other things you wanted to do."

Amara gasped. "*You* talked to Brandon?"

"I did. He seems like a smart young man with good business sense. I trust him."

Out of the corner of her eye, she could see Daisy moving

side to side, obviously trying to contain her excitement. And while Amara was just as excited, the idea that her parents trusted Brandon more than her stung.

Why couldn't they trust her the same way?

Just be happy that you're getting to bake what you want to bake again.

She *was* happy. Thrilled even. And to show it, she ran around the counter and hugged her dad. Daisy squealed and ran to hug him on his other side—making him the middle of their giddy girl sandwich.

He managed to wiggle out of their clutches eventually, and Amara calmed down enough to tell him, "Thank you, Dad. This means a lot and I promise I won't let you down again."

"*De nada*. Just remember that this isn't a pass to go crazy and change everything. I still own this bakery so I need to be involved with the decisions, okay?"

"Okay."

"And I guess when I get back home I'll call Eric to let him know."

Amara's spirit deflated a little. She wanted to be the one to tell Eric. "I'll tell him," she blurted. "That way I can go over the plans again. He's supposed to stop by later to drop off some, um, supplies."

"Fine, you do it. We'll talk about everything else tonight after dinner. Your mother is going to want you to...is that *capirotada*?" He walked back to the counter and bent to smell the casserole dish.

"It is," Amara said with a smile.

"But it's not Friday."

"I know. I just felt like making it today. You can take the

rest home if you want. Daisy and I already ate too much of it."

"Speak for yourself," Daisy said.

"Well, we already had lunch and your mom is taking a nap. I guess I can take it and we can have it later for dessert."

"Sure, Dad. Go ahead."

Her dad picked up the casserole dish and started to walk toward the door. She covered her mouth to stifle a giggle, though, when he hesitated then came back to grab one of the forks from the plates still on the counter. When he left, she noticed he didn't cross the street toward their house, but instead turned right and continued walking down the sidewalk. She estimated it would take him about ten minutes to finish what was left in the casserole before going back home.

Daisy clapped and hugged her again. "Wow, Amara. I can't believe this is happening. What do you think Brandon said that convinced them to change their minds so fast?"

She'd wondered the same thing. "I don't know, but I'm going to ask him right now."

Amara grabbed her phone and called Brandon. He answered after two rings.

"Hey there, new business partner," he said.

"Is this for real? I still can't believe it."

"Well, believe it. Starting next month, your fabulous desserts are going on the weekend menu at L.A. Cuchara."

"Gosh, Brandon. I don't even know what to say. First of all, I can't believe that my dad called you to set this up."

"Oh, he didn't call me. I called him."

"What?"

"I don't know if you've realized this about me yet, but I don't really like to take no for an answer when it comes to business deals. When you told me you couldn't go through with our agreement because your parents wouldn't sign off on it, I figured I needed to meet with them myself and let them know that my proposal was serious. So I invited them to lunch today at my restaurant."

Amara walked over to the plastic chairs and sat down. "I can't believe they went!'

"Oh, yeah. They loved it. I made sure they got the VIP treatment, and I had my sister make a couple of her specialty dishes just for them. Seriously, her *arroz con pollo* is freaking amazing."

"And that was it? You gave them a great lunch and then they were ready to sign on the dotted line?"

"Well, not exactly. I talked to them for a long time and told them how I thought this partnership would take the bakery to a new level of popularity. And when I knew I had them, that's when I threw out the ultimatum."

"Which was?"

"The agreement was only going to happen if they gave you control of the menu and the entire remodel project. I told them that I was basically referring my celebrity clients to your bakery and that meant it had to meet certain expectations."

"And that did it?"

"Pretty much. Your mom was in as soon as I mentioned a few of the Mexican actors and singers who always come in, and that they had a table right next to them whenever they wanted. And your dad, well, he was looking for a pen once I mentioned tickets to one of the World Cup qualifying games next year."

Amara couldn't quite process her shock. The partnership

was real. "Unbelievable. Thank you so much, Brandon. I don't even know how I can repay you."

"Just make me some amazing desserts. We're partners now, Amara. And that means my success is your success and vice versa. So get ready, because your life is about to change."

Her throat knotted and tears wet her eyes. Happiness couldn't even begin to describe the emotion she was feeling. Her dream was actually going to happen. She was finally going to get what she wanted.

Thoughts turned to Eric and she knew he'd be just as excited as she was. The expanded remodel meant more work for him and more time for the two of them to be together—something else she'd been wanting for a while but never had the courage to tell him.

Until now.

She had to find the perfect moment to bring up the idea of them continuing to see each other even after the remodel was done.

And she knew just how to do it.

Chapter Sixteen

Eric checked his backpack one more time. There were socks, an extra pair of boxer briefs, a pair of jeans, two T-shirts, his toothbrush and toothpaste, and condoms. Lots of condoms.

All of the essentials he'd need for his first overnight date with Amara.

She'd surprised him earlier in the week by telling him that she booked a room for them at a downtown hotel for Sunday night. His dick had been hard for nearly four days just thinking about it, especially since she'd stayed away from him all week. She'd told him that she was busy helping Daisy get ready for one of her parties, but he could tell something else was up.

He was planning to get it out of her tonight. But only after all of the sex.

Eric slung his backpack over his shoulder just as his cell phone rang. He looked down and his eyebrows shot up. He brought the phone to his ear. "Hey Sal, long time no talk."

"Oh, so you *do* remember me? I was starting to think you lost my number...on purpose."

Sal Benavides had been Eric's main project site manager. It had killed him to have to let Sal go when the company started to bleed money, but his friend had understood and was able to find another job pretty quickly. Sal had even tried to get Eric on the same job but it never worked out, and then Eric left for East L.A. He hadn't talked to him since.

"Nah, it's not like that," Eric told him. "I've just been busy. How's it going?"

"Pretty good, actually. That's why I'm calling."

Eric threw his backpack onto a nearby chair and sat on his bed. "What do you mean?"

"Well, I just got hired on as the site manager for a new condo project just outside the Strip. I'm able to bring in some of my own guys for this and I wanted to know if you wanted a spot. It's a guaranteed gig for at least a year. What do you say?"

Eric stood up and paced his small room. A call like this had been what he'd been waiting for. The chance to get back into the big time, to rebuild his name...and earn enough money to jumpstart his company.

So why wasn't he saying yes?

"Wow, thanks man. I appreciate you thinking of me."

"So is that a yes?"

"Well, it's just that I'm in the middle of another job right now and I probably won't be finished for awhile." That wasn't exactly true. He'd probably be done in three weeks.

"That's no problem. I wouldn't need you on site for another two months at least. You can finish up that job, tie up any loose ends, and then come back to Vegas. You can stay on my couch until you find a new place."

Eric's head spun. Sal was offering him the perfect chance to put the next phase of his plan into action. There were a thousand reasons why he should take it.

And only one why he shouldn't.

"Can I think about it for a few days?" He closed his eyes when he said it, afraid to hear the answer.

Sal sighed through the phone. "Uh, I guess. But are you hesitating because you got something better going on over there?"

"No, I don't have any better jobs lined up here." That was definitely true.

"So what's the issue? If it's money, you know I'm going to do right by you. Don't even worry about it."

"I know that. It's not the money."

"Then what's keeping you down there in L.A.?"

Eric didn't answer because he wasn't quite sure how to explain it. Instead, he thanked Sal again for the opportunity and promised he'd call him back in a couple of days.

A few weeks ago, this would've been a no-brainer. Leaving his *abuela* would be hard, of course, but it wouldn't be like before. This time he'd make an effort to visit a few times a month and give his mom money to hire a nurse to take care of her during the day, so that wasn't the reason he was thinking of turning Sal down.

But this thing with Amara is going to end in a few weeks anyway.

Maybe. Maybe not. They'd grown closer and, for him at least, it was more than just sexual. They'd become friends again. Maybe more.

If he left now, there was no chance he'd know for sure.

Eric grabbed his backpack and headed for the door. He couldn't think about Sal or Vegas right now. All he wanted to do was spend one very long night with Amara.

And, hopefully, their time together would help him make a decision once and for all.

Chapter Seventeen

Amara blinked at the image staring back at her from the full-length mirror attached to the bathroom door—the face of a woman ready to have sex. Was she imagining the sheen of her dark hair, pink flush of her cheeks, or fullness of her lips?

She was definitely dressed for the occasion. She'd splurged on a baby-doll nightie that perfectly accentuated the roundness of her cleavage, yet hid the roundness of her middle. The sheer black nylon teased only shadows of her nipples and the dark vee between her thighs. She turned around and looked over her shoulder. The fur-edged hem of the garment barely covered the curves of her bottom.

Although she told herself she'd never be a vixen, Amara had to admit that, standing there in her see-through hundred and twenty dollar nightie, she looked sexy. The feel of her growing arousal surprised her, but she shocked herself even more when she moved her hand to one breast and started caressing and squeezing. Watching herself fondle herself only excited her more and she couldn't help but reach under the nightgown and slide one finger over her clit.

If there hadn't been a sexy, virile man waiting for her on the other side of the door, Amara would have gotten herself off right there. The personal moment of her foreplay had done the job of getting her all hot and bothered—and horny enough to do whatever it was that Eric wanted to do.

Scratch that. It was time to make Eric do whatever *she* wanted to do. Pushing the hotel bathroom door open, she took a deep breath.

He was sitting on the bed, his back straight up against the black vinyl headboard. "Turn around," he commanded.

Slowly, she turned in a circle and she heard him hiss. "Fuck, you're so beautiful." The hoarseness of his voice surprised and pleased her.

"Do you like?" she said with a drawl.

"I'll like it more after ripping it off you."

She made her way to the bed and crawled like a cat alongside his body, sleek and slow. Her gaze locked on his. Intense. Bare. His eyes had transformed into dark pools of desire and they pushed her into new, uncharted depths of wanting. No more wavering. No more hesitation.

Amara knew exactly what she wanted. She had some good news to share and she'd eventually tell him over dinner. But first she wanted dessert.

Reaching over with her right hand, she cupped his jaw and brushed her index finger over his lips. His eyes widened at the lingering scent of her arousal. His mouth opened and she slid her finger inside. "You tasted me. Now I'm going to taste you," she told him, her voice thick with desire. She kissed and licked her way down his broad chest and hard abdomen. When she reached his briefs, she hooked her fingers on the sides and slid them down over his muscled thighs and calves. She curled her fingers around his thick shaft. It was hot to the touch and she could feel the blood pulsing through the engorged veins. Her fingers slid up, then down its length. A bead of moisture gathered at the tip and she bowed her head and licked it up. Eric's moans increased her confidence and desire.

When she finally took all of him in her mouth, Eric jerked as if he had been electrocuted. "Oh, God," he groaned and tangled his fingers in her hair.

She continued sucking and licking, increasing her rhythm.

"Shit, Amara. I can't take any more. Condom. Now."

She slid the condom out from under the pillow where she'd stashed it, rolled it into place while he watched her with heated eyes, and then straddled his legs. Eric raised an eyebrow.

"Tonight, I'm on top," she said, and sank down onto him.

His loud moan drowned out her sigh. "Fuck, yeah, sweetheart," he gritted out. "Fuck me *good*."

His words ignited her and she started moving with purpose. His face contorted with pleasure, building the satisfaction growing inside her. She'd never felt so powerful. So in control. Eric did that to her. Whether it was encouraging her to take over the bakery or to give in to her sexual urges, he made it safe for her to finally take what she wanted. And it thrilled her to no end. She threw her head back in wild abandon and rode him until her sex clenched and she tumbled over the edge with a keening cry.

"God, you're beautiful when you come," he rasped from beneath her. "And although I love the view of those breasts bouncing up and down, it's *my* turn to fuck *you*."

In one swift move, he was on top of her. His mouth slammed against hers, ravaging her tongue, then her neck, and finally her breasts. He nudged her thighs open with his knee and she felt his erection, hot and thick against her thigh. She raised her head to possess his lips once again. They both groaned, grabbing and clawing each other as their kisses turned savage. The peaks of her hardened nipples brushed against his chest, sending her pleasure climbing once more. The need to have him inside her again made her crazy with wild abandon. Nothing mattered more.

"Now, Eric. *Now*," she moaned into his mouth.

He pulled away and she could see that desire in his eyes, and her heart soared. "Are you ready for me?"

"Yes, oh God, please, yes."

His first thrust was hard and deep and they both gasped. Instant pleasure. Then he started to move, slow and methodical. He lowered his body and took one of her nipples in his mouth. The sensation of him inside her combined with his nibbles and licks on her breasts were almost too much. She needed to come.

He continued pumping into her, spreading her legs as far as he could in order to bury himself as deep as possible. She dug her nails into his arms and they crashed together— their combined pleasure creating a smile on her face and warmth in her heart.

Her life had changed so much since Eric had walked back into it. They were good together in and out of bed. That had to mean something, didn't it?

Amara decided she couldn't be afraid anymore to find out.

• • •

Eric couldn't remember the last time he'd felt so full...or so happy. Amara had given him hours of mind-blowing sex. Then they'd devoured a delicious dinner at a tiny hole-in-the wall restaurant in Chinatown.

It made the phone call with Sal that much harder to ignore.

He took a drink of his water and tried to clear his mind. For Amara's sake. Clearly they were celebrating something big, and it wasn't every day he got to spend the entire night with her. Hell, this was the first. If anything could block out the offer in Vegas, it was thinking of how much he would enjoy feasting on Amara again as soon as they got back to the hotel room.

But first, to figure out what they were celebrating.

"Okay, so now that dinner's over, are you going to tell me why we're here? Don't get me wrong, I've loved every single minute of tonight, but I can tell you're ready to burst with your big news. So spill it."

An enormous grin spread across her face. "Okay, so you're not going to believe this but my parents are going to let me go ahead with my plans to revamp the bakery's menu and we're going to hold a huge grand re-opening event next month! Isn't that amazing!"

Eric's heart soared. He'd never seen her so happy. And that made him happy as well.

"That's amazing!" That seemed like quite a turnaround

for Ricardo and Consuelo, though. Something wasn't adding up. "So what changed? What made them get on board with everything?"

"Brandon did. Brandon convinced them!"

His muscles tensed. "What do you mean?"

"After I told him I couldn't sign the agreement because I wasn't the official owner of the bakery, he called my dad and met with them on his own. Can you believe it?"

"Sounds like they liked him."

"Of course, they did. Who wouldn't? And the moment he started name-dropping, they were impressed. So when he mentioned that he wanted to help promote the bakery to his celebrity customers and the offer was only good if they implemented my ideas— "

"They agreed," he finished for her.

Her smile faded a bit at the edges. "I'm not going to lie. It's a lot of pressure. Brandon has faith in me but my parents still don't. They're not willing to sell me the bakery yet. But if I can prove to them that I can turn Brandon's investment into a success, maybe they'll come around."

He smiled. "They will. I know it."

"I hope so." She leaned forward, her expression filling with excitement all over again. "God, Eric. This is huge. I never thought I'd get this chance again. I'll never be able to repay Brandon for this!"

Amara continued to gush about how Brandon had saved the day. On one hand, he was happy that she was going to be able to run the bakery the way she'd dreamed. On the other, he wanted to be the one who made that dream come true. And he hadn't. And couldn't.

Sure, he could build a few cabinets and hang a few

pieces of drywall. But at the end of the day, it took money to give Amara what she needed. What she deserved. And until he could start his construction company and become a businessman just like Brandon, she'd never consider being with him for longer than an overnight hotel stay.

"Why are you so quiet?" Her voice brought him back to the restaurant. "I just said this means you'll get to expand the remodel like we talked about. And you still have a job for a few more weeks, so I was thinking we could still hang out?"

Eric went still. His friend has asked him what was tying him to L.A. and he hadn't been able to answer him because he didn't know.

Now he did. There's wasn't anything keeping him here after all.

Amara had seen the opportunity to expand the remodel as an opportunity to expand their time together, which was great…except she was obviously still planning to end things by the bakery's grand re-opening. And when things were over, he'd be back exactly where he started.

With nothing.

He'd been so distracted with helping her realize her dream that he'd forgotten about his. Since when did Eric Valencia put a woman's needs before his own? It was time to start thinking about his future—a future that didn't include Amara.

"Is something wrong?"

"What? No, of course not. I told you I'm happy for you. I am." He tried to smile, but failed. "Turns out, I have some news of my own. I may have a new construction job lined up. In Vegas."

Her face went blank. "What do you mean?"

"I got a call this morning from my buddy. He's got a spot on his crew for a big condo project and he wants me to take it. If I do, then I need to leave next month."

It was obvious she was surprised. Beyond that, her emotions were unknown. "But what about...your *abuela*?" she finally asked.

He cleared his throat and tried to look anywhere but into her beautiful eyes. Eyes he knew would shred him to the core. "I know it's going to be hard to leave her, but I think this will really be good for me."

She sat back in her chair. "Sounds like you've got it all figured out."

He dismissed her tone. He couldn't afford to think about whether she disapproved of his decision. Time to change the subject to something they both could agree on, and perhaps the one thing they'd ever have in common. Sex.

"I'm still weighing all my options, but that's enough talk about our work. Let's get the check and then get back to our room. I'm feeling hungry again."

She smiled at his comment. Not as big as when she'd told him about Brandon but he'd take it. In fact, he'd take whatever she gave him at this point.

Because in a few weeks, there'd be nothing.

Chapter Eighteen

She hated being one of those girls.

But when she picked up her cell phone—yet again—to make sure she didn't have a missed call from Eric, she couldn't deny that she was, in fact, one of those girls.

Amara went back to making tracks in her mashed potatoes with her fork as her parents discussed whether there would be enough leftovers of the roast chicken for their lunch tomorrow.

It had been two days since she'd heard from or seen Eric. She couldn't shake the feeling that something changed the other night at dinner. And not in the way she'd hoped.

"Are you done?" Her mother's question interrupted her mind-wandering. Looking down at her half-eaten chicken breast, flattened mashed potatoes, and newly-stabbed pieces of green beans, Amara nodded. Her mother picked up her plate and disappeared into the kitchen.

After checking one more time that her phone hadn't

rung without her hearing it, she looked at her dad from across the table. Well, she looked at the newspaper he now held up in front of his face. "Have you heard from Eric recently?"

"No," he said from behind the *Deportes* section. "I just figured he's been working some late nights trying to finish up some things. Why?"

"Just wondering. I had a few questions for him, that's all."

"Why don't you call him? I have his number if you need it."

So do I. "No, that's okay. I don't want to bother him if he's sleeping. I'll just leave a note for him at the bakery tomorrow."

As she lay in her bed later that night, unanswered questions and lingering doubts refused to let her sleep.

She punched her pillow a few times, trying to get comfortable. Sure, Eric hadn't called but that didn't mean things were over. Not yet. And certainly not without telling her face-to-face. She wouldn't let herself believe that he'd ever do that to her. She meant something to him, didn't she? Even as she tried to convince herself that he hadn't disappeared without a word all over again, the restlessness wouldn't go away. And so she lay there. Tossing and turning. Wondering and waiting.

Frustration turned to irritation until she'd had enough. Playing silly mind games was for teenagers. There was no reason why she couldn't just pick up the phone and demand to know what was going on.

She threw off the sheet, shot out of bed, and grabbed her phone. It was already after eleven. She punched in his number and waited.

He answered after only one ring.

"It's Amara. Before you say anything I need you to listen. First of all, I know I might've seemed a little weird about you going back to Vegas but then we had sex and I thought everything was okay. But if you decided to leave early for some reason, it's kind of crappy of you not to at least call to tell me. No hard feelings. Just don't be a jerk about it and jerk me around because— "

"Stop, Amara. Just stop."

"I'm not done talking. Remember you're supposed to be listening. I deserve at least that, I think. Can you give me— "

"I said stop already! I haven't called you because I've been at the hospital. My *abuela* is dying."

. . .

The beat of the monitor played on. Like a tune you couldn't get out of your head, it was a tormenting kind of obsession.

Except this melody let Eric know that his grandmother was still alive. Barely.

He looked at her sleeping in the hospital bed, wires and tubes running from different parts of her body up to those monitors. The second attack had been much stronger—much more devastating on her heart. The doctors delivered the grim prognosis the previous night—his grandma had days, maybe hours left.

"The nurses said I can stay here tonight," his mom said as she came back into the room. "So I'm going to go home and get some things. Can you stay here until I get back?"

"Of course."

"Good. But you call me if anything changes, okay?"

"I will."

"Don't say anything that will upset her."

"What's that supposed to mean?"

"I just mean she needs to rest and it's not good for her to get upset."

"And you think I'm such a horrible grandson that I'd purposefully do something like that? Thanks a lot, Mom." He stood up and stalked out of the room.

He'd reached the elevator by the time his mom caught up with him. "Hey, where are you going? I thought you were going to stay with her?"

"I will. I just need some air."

The elevator doors opened and he walked inside. His mother followed. "I don't think you're a horrible grandson," she said.

"Could've fooled me," he told her.

"I just...I'm trying..." Her voice broke. "I'm sorry." And then his mother started sobbing. The obvious pain in her cries twisted his heart until he couldn't take it anymore. He grabbed her and held her close until the elevator doors opened.

Still holding her, he guided them outside the hospital and to a concrete bench. She sat down and pulled a tissue from her jacket pocket. He took a seat next to her. "I'm sorry, too. For everything."

She shook her head and blew her nose. "I know I've been hard on you since you came back. You didn't deserve that."

"But I did. I do."

She grabbed his hand. "I shouldn't have kicked you out.

I was wrong. And I'm sorry it's taken me so long to say it. When she's gone, all we're going to have is each other…"

Her tears came again, and this time his own threatened to fall. His *abuela* was going to die. Guilt tugged at him. It couldn't have been easy for her to see him and his mom fighting all of the time. He owed it to her to make these last few days as peaceful as possible. It was time to let go of the past.

"We do have each other, Mom. I'm here for whatever you need."

Eventually, her tears stopped and she left to go to the house to pick up her things. He made his way back to the room and sat in the recliner next to his *abuela*'s hospital bed.

He had started to nod off when his pocket vibrated. He didn't have to pull his phone out to know that it was Amara calling…again. She was worried about him, but he couldn't think about that now.

"*Mijo*?"

Eric scooted his chair closer to the bed and grabbed his *abuela*'s hand. "I'm here."

Weary eyes met his worried ones. She looked so small and frail. He couldn't stand it.

"*Agua*?" she asked, her voice cracking.

He nodded and stood up to pour her a small cup of water. Gently, he helped her lift her head so she could take a sip. Then she lay back down and smiled at him.

"Why are you still here? The bakery…"

"That can wait. I need to be here with you and Mom."

"Diana?"

"She went home to get a few things. She's going to stay overnight with you. The nurses said it would be okay."

His *abuela* nodded her head and grabbed his hand again. "Need you. Do something for me."

He tried not to wince as she struggled for each word. Each breath. "Of course. Anything."

"Take care...your mother. She's stubborn...like you. That's why you fight. The same."

"I promise."

"Good. Something...else."

"Something else?"

"Robles girl."

"Amara? What do you mean?"

"Be with her."

"What?"

"You like her. She like you. Be with her."

He smiled. He could never hide anything from her. But his smile didn't last. "Her family doesn't think I'm good enough for her. Maybe they're right."

"*Basta!*" Her outburst ended in a coughing fit. He grabbed the cup and helped her take another drink. When she was done, he tried to tell her to save her strength and rest, but she wasn't having any of that. His *abuela* needed to talk, and a failing heart wasn't about to stop her from saying what she had to say.

"No more. Yes, you make mistakes long time ago. But you...good man. She...good woman. No matter anything else."

Tears welled up, and his throat knotted with grief. After everything he had put her through, his *abuela* still believed in him. The question was, could he believe in himself once she was gone? He squeezed her hand and watched her drift back to sleep. The monitors told him she hadn't left him yet.

So he sat back in his chair, covered his face with his hands and finally let the tears escape.

• • •

The funeral Mass of *Doña* Arroyo was as beautiful as it was sad. Amara couldn't help but be affected when Father Marcos talked about her love of God and family.

Amara knew that *Doña* Arroyo—before her attack— had been one of a handful of women responsible for cleaning the small church, cooking for Fr. Marcos and cutting flowers from the rectory's garden to place on the altar every week. She didn't just go to this church, she took care of it. And now it was time for it to take care of her.

"Her legacy of love and faith will continue to live in those who knew her and those who loved her," the father said.

Those like her grandson Eric.

She watched from her seat toward the back as he walked with his *abuela's* coffin down the aisle, along with five other men she didn't recognize. A need to run to him, to comfort him, overwhelmed her, so much so that she had to wrap her arms around herself to keep from doing something that would raise eyebrows and questions.

But if he saw Amara, he didn't acknowledge her. Instead, he kept his shoulders squared and eyes straight ahead for the entire service. She tried to catch his attention at the cemetery, but people constantly flanked him on either side, patting his back and shaking his hand, offering their condolences. The community that had shunned him now embraced him.

If she had any hope of talking to him at the luncheon held afterward in the church's multipurpose hall, it was dashed soon after she arrived to deliver the *besos* she'd made especially for the occasion. He was nowhere to be found.

She walked into the small kitchen to leave the tray of pastries and bumped into Eric's mom, who was on her way out. Then the woman she barely knew proceeded to break down right in front of her.

Amara set the tray down on the counter and reached over to pat her shoulder. "I'm so sorry for your loss. She was an amazing woman."

Diana Valencia nodded and then tried to compose herself by wiping her eyes and pulling a tissue from her watchband to blow her nose. "Thank you, Amara. She really liked you."

"She did? I think I really only talked to her that one time in the bakery."

"Well, Eric talked about you and everything you were doing for your parents. And she would always tell him that you were something special."

Amara could feel her cheeks burn. She had no idea she was a conversation topic in Eric's home. Speaking of Eric...

"He's not here," Diana said as she busied herself with setting out more plates and napkins for the food. "My son is taking this very hard. The funeral was too much for him so he went home."

"Oh. That's too bad. I never got a chance to tell him...to offer my sympathies."

Diana walked over to her and grabbed both of her hands. "He says he's okay, but I know he's not," she said, her eyes full of sadness and more tears. "He won't talk to me. Maybe he'll talk to you?"

She stood there in stunned silence as Eric's mother took a set of keys from her pocket and handed it to her. "It's the big silver one," she said, and then walked out of the kitchen.

Without stopping to analyze choices or weigh consequences, Amara gripped the keys and walked out of the hall. When she got to the sidewalk in front of the church, she started to run.

Everything was a blur of houses and cars as she made her way down the one block to Eric's house. She landed, breathless, on his doorstep, anxious and shaking so badly she could barely get the key into the lock. She walked through the small house until she came to his bedroom's closed door. He was in there. She knew it in her gut. She opened the door.

He was lying on his back on his bed with his hands underneath his head. But as soon as he saw her, his face crumpled and he covered his eyes with his arms.

"Please, Amara, go away." His voice cracked.

Her heart broke. His grief was palpable. So was his need.

She closed the door behind her, turned the lock and joined him on the bed. At first he tried to turn away from her, but she wouldn't let him and brought his arms down to his side.

Gently, she kissed his forehead and brushed the sides of his hair with her fingers. His cheeks were wet, from his tears or hers she didn't know. But she kissed them, too. He opened his eyes to whisper, "What are you doing?"

"I'm taking away your pain," she answered against his lips. At first, he didn't respond to her light kisses. She worried that he would push her off of him or be angry that she didn't leave him like he'd asked. But he didn't push her way. Instead, he wrapped his arms around her and buried his face into her shoulder.

They held each other until the sun went down. At some

point, she'd moved her head down against his chest and lain there listening to his heartbeat, anticipating every breath. If it weren't for his fingers combing through her hair every now and then, she might have thought he'd fallen asleep.

Her own eyes grew heavy but she fought to stay awake in case he wanted to talk.

And eventually he did.

"I can't believe she's gone," he said into the darkness. "You know, I woke up this morning and the first thing I thought was, 'I wonder if *abuela* wants to go the grocery store today.' Then I remembered."

She felt a tear slide from the corner of her eye and down the side of her face onto his shirt. "I'm so sorry, Eric. I know how much she meant to you."

"What am I going to do without her, Amara?" his voice was thick with emotion.

"You go on. And you live your life knowing that she loved you and that she was proud of you."

She didn't know if those were the words he wanted to hear. But it was truth. And if the words didn't bring him some comfort, she could only hope that her touch would. Reaching across his chest, she found his hand and linked her fingers through his.

"Thank you for staying with me," he said after awhile. "I bet everyone is wondering where you are."

"Let them wonder. I'm here for as long as you need me to be."

And that's when she knew this thing with Eric was more than just sex. He'd become important to her, to her life. Maybe, just maybe, there didn't have to be an end for them.

Chapter Nineteen

"It's perfect. Just perfect."

Eric's heart surged. Amara spun in a circle, taking in the finishing touches he'd put on the renovation late last night. Her eyes glistened with tears and he knew he'd done well. At last.

It had been three weeks since his *abuela's* funeral and life had moved on. It had to. The bakery needed to be finished. He couldn't let Amara and her family down.

He'd worked around the clock over the past few days, making Amara promise not to go inside until he came back after his meeting with the lawyer to discuss his a*buela's* will. He'd even blindfolded her outside before letting her in.

Now as she walked in circles, surveying the renovated bakery, the joy and lightness that filled her face gave him such satisfaction.

"I can't wait to see all of this filled up with your sweet desserts," he said and grabbed her around the waist from behind and rested his chin on her shoulder.

"You really did it. You gave me my dream."

His heart soared. Even if it wasn't true, she'd said *he* gave her the dream. Not Brandon, *him*. He kissed her on the cheek and then spun her around. "This is all you, Amara. All I did was put the pieces where you told me to put them. You gave yourself your dream."

"So tell me. What happened with the lawyer?"

He grabbed her hands tight. "Well, it was like we thought. She left my mom the house. My mom wants to sell it. She says it will be too hard to live there without *abuela*. She's always wanted to move to Oregon so that's what she's going to do. She's going to give me half of whatever she makes on the house."

"That's good, right?"

Although he was grateful for the money, it didn't take away from his continuing sadness. "I guess."

"Hey, what happened to that smile?" Amara grabbed his face with her hands and searched his eyes.

He shrugged. "I don't know. The money will help, for sure. But I'd give it back in a minute to have her back."

"I know. I know." She wrapped her arms around him and he took comfort in her warmth. When he finally let go, she said "What if you use the money on something she would've wanted?"

"What do you mean?"

"You said your *abuela* always wanted you to go to college, so do that. Go back to school."

"What? You're joking, right?"

"Nope. I'm not saying apply to a four-year university. But maybe you could take some classes at a junior college or a trade school? This is your second chance. Take it."

He couldn't think of one single reason why he shouldn't. "I *have* always wanted to take some business management classes. I could use part of the money for tuition and put away the rest until I'm ready to start my own construction company."

"You want to start your own company?"

He rubbed the back of his neck. "Well, yeah. I'm tired of relying on other people to find me work. I know it's going to take some time before I can be my own boss. But it will be easier taking on these temp jobs because I'll know it won't be like that forever. So now I just need to figure out school. I guess I can do it online, or I think Las Vegas has a pretty good community college…"

She frowned and took a step back. "Wait. Las Vegas?"

"I told you about that job offer, remember?"

"Yes. But for some reason I thought you were still going to look here in L.A.?"

"I was, but this is a guaranteed gig. I have to take what I can get."

She shook her head. "I'm sure if you ask my brother, he'd be happy to give you some contacts."

"Probably. But I really need to do this on my own."

What he didn't tell her was that he'd already asked Miguel. But his friend had pressed him hard for reasons as to why he wanted to stay in L.A. He didn't feel comfortable saying anything about Amara for obvious reasons, but also because he wasn't sure what to do with their relationship. Did she want more? Did he?

There was no better time than the present to find out.

"I can still come down on the weekends to see you,"

he offered. "There's a pretty decent motel down the street where we could…"

She put her hands on her hips—hips he wanted to grab hold of and not let go until she was screaming his name. "And what? Have a weekend booty call?"

Wait, no. He frowned. "That's not what I meant. I just meant we could spend some time together alone."

"I don't know…"

"Look, Amara. I'm trying here. Just tell me what you want." Truth was he wanted her to tell him to stay—to give him hope that one day she could learn to love him.

Like the way that he already loved her.

The realization fell onto his chest like a piece of cement block—knocking the wind out of his lungs and striking terror in his heart. He loved her. Of course he did. But should he tell her? If he did, it would change everything. Forever.

"I want things to stay how they are," she finally said. "I don't understand why you can't find something here and we can keep on doing what we've been doing."

He folded his arms across his chest. "Until when?"

She hesitated. "What do you mean?"

"I mean it's time to tell me where you see this—us—going."

"I… I don't know." She turned away, her arms wrapping around her middle, and moved toward the windows in front of the bakery.

Old defenses rose up. What if she *did* know, but didn't want to tell him? Maybe he'd been all wrong about what had been growing between them? No, he told himself. He knew there was something there; he'd been feeling it for weeks. It was time for her to admit it.

And if she couldn't?

Then you know what happens next.

"Why can't you just say it?" he pressed.

"Say what? Why is this such a big deal?"

"Because it is!" He didn't mean to yell at her, so he took a breath before starting again. "You still don't know what you want—or you're too afraid to admit it. And if that's the case, then I'm sorry, but there comes a point where maybe I just need to stop asking you."

It was partly true. He loved her, but he couldn't be with someone who couldn't even tell her parents that they were together. If he stayed he was risking his future—his sobriety—on someone who could hurt him deep. Deeper than anyone ever had before.

"So what's it going to be?" He was pushing now, but he didn't care.

She whirled around and glared at him, her hands fisted at her sides. "Why is this up to me? If you really wanted to stay then you'd stay. Don't you *dare* make this my decision."

Did she not care one way or the other? "If I go, I'm not coming back. Is that what you really want?"

"Does it even matter? Did it ever?"

Her words punched him in the gut. Hard. "Of course it does. Dammit, Amara! Isn't that what this—us—was all about?"

She clenched her fists and marched across the room, stopping right in front of him. "What do you want me to say, Eric? We both agreed this was just about sex. We both knew it couldn't ever be more than that because Trina told me that you didn't come back here looking for a girlfriend. Plus, I'm so close to taking over the bakery. I can't risk it now for something that's just going to end later."

And there it was. He'd agreed to sex and *only* sex, and now he was expecting her to feel the same way he did. She was right. He braced himself for the question he didn't want to ask. "So this is over?"

"I guess so."

There were no more words to say. She'd made it clear what she wanted. And it wasn't him. So he turned around and walked out of the bakery, and away from Amara for the last time.

Chapter Twenty

Never in her baking career would Amara have thought she'd be crying over spilled water. Yet, there she was, bawling like a baby after accidentally tipping her water bottle over and onto a tray of freshly baked *orejas*. Water began to seep over some of the ear-shaped pastries, turning their sugar-coated flaky goodness into soggy, malformed messes.

They were drowning. Just like her.

It had been three days since Eric told her he was going back to Vegas. She'd been angry at first, angry enough to tell him the bakery was more important to her than he was. And when he walked out the door, it took everything she had not to go running after him and tell him she wanted him to stay.

But she couldn't bring herself to do it. Couldn't risk it. If her parents knew about her and Eric they'd surely pull out of their agreement with Brandon, using the excuse that she'd lied to them all of this time. Brandon had invested his trust—and his money—in Amara. She'd failed her parents before by wasting their money on the cupcake shop. She wasn't about to do it all over again. She owed it to them, to Brandon, to everyone to make sure this plan to reinvent the bakery went off without a hitch.

So she'd let Eric go.

The night he left, numbness spread throughout her body like a flu virus, leaving her tired, listless, and without an appetite. She'd spent the next few days in an absent-minded fog, forgetting things like where she put her keys or whether she needed two cups of flour or three for her anise gingerbread cookies. Then this morning, while taking a shower, she began to cry. Actually, not just cry, but wail. With her hair still caked in shampoo, she crumpled into the corner of the bathtub, her pain and heartbreak thankfully muffled by the jets of water cascading down around her.

Eventually, she managed somehow to leave the tub, get dressed, and walk to the bakery just as the sun was coming up over the rows of homes on the hilly, tree-lined streets. And when her thoughts threatened to pull her back into that sorrowful abyss, she just punched the dough harder or whisked the eggs faster.

But all it took was that one spill for the torrent of emotions she'd been trying to smother to come crashing back with a vengeance. The hysterical wave carried her from the middle of the kitchen into the dark pantry where she fell back against the shelves and sobbed into her hands. Loss, grief, emptiness. They were inside each tear that fell. So she let herself cry until her soul had been emptied and all her tears used up. Exactly how long she sat there, Amara didn't know. But it wasn't until she heard a deep voice calling her name that she scrambled to her feet.

The voice yelled again. *Crap!* It was Brandon. Vaguely, she remembered him calling last night to ask if he could stop by today to give her something.

"Just a second, please. I'll be right out," she called back. She needed to clean herself up but she was trapped. There wasn't a wall between the front of the bakery and the bathroom anymore so she couldn't run in there without him seeing her. Looking around the kitchen, she spotted her large, shiny, not-yet-used spatula and grabbed it. Holding it up in front of her, Amara angled the impromptu mirror to check her reflection. Even in the blurriness of the metal, she could tell she looked like a disaster—a puffy, red-eyed disaster.

She sighed.

It didn't matter. Brandon probably cared less than she did about how she looked anyway. So she blew her nose into a paper towel, smoothed her hair down and plastered on a smile.

"There you are," he said as she walked out to meet him. "I thought maybe you had locked yourself in a freezer or something. Or does that only happen on TV shows?"

"Well, my freezer isn't that big. So unless I accidentally fall into it somehow, I don't imagine you ever having to rescue me from it."

"Good to know. Although I doubt you're the kind of woman who would ever need a man to rescue her. It seems to me like you're pretty capable all on your own," he said with a wink.

A year ago, she would've melted at that wink. Today, it barely made her smile. "Wow. Compliments and a gift? You should visit more often."

"That's right." He reached into the inside pocket of his

suit jacket and pulled out an envelope and handed it her. "Open it."

The twinkle in his eyes made her narrow hers. What was he so excited about?

She lifted the envelope's flap and slid out what she could tell was another check. There was really no need to look at the amount. It was the balance of his first payment. Still, she glanced down and discovered a very different number...and blinked. Twice.

"What?"

"I decided to give you a deposit for the rest of the year."

"Why?" Apparently the shock had rendered her only able to speak single words.

"Something tells me you're going to be very, very busy soon and I wanted to guarantee a longer partnership."

"Huh?" Lord. It was like she was a cavewoman.

"There's something else inside the envelope. Take a look." The mischievous glint and silly grin were back.

With trembling hands, she slid out two rectangular cards. They looked like concert tickets but when she brought them closer to read, she realized they had nothing to do with music. They were passes to the very popular, already sold-out Southern California Food and Wine Festival set for the following month.

"How?" Again with the one-word sentences. So embarrassing.

"You're coming as my guest, and you'll also be part of the tasting event. Well, not you specifically, but your desserts. And I figured that once people discover your bakery, you'll have your hands full."

The tears that wet her eyes came from happiness this

time, but she blinked them back, careful not to let any—happy or not—sneak past the floodgates again. "This is amazing. *You* are amazing. I don't know what else to say except 'thank you.'"

"That's enough for me. Well that and maybe one of those chocolate crepe things I've been eyeing since I got here."

After tucking the check and the tickets safely back into the envelope, she placed it next to the register and pet it like a cat. She would open it again later and probably jump around like crazy after Brandon left. Right now, though, she needed to get that crepe.

As she watched him devour it, pure gratitude welled up inside her. Attending the Food and Wine Festival could be the break she needed to turn the bakery around. And the extra money would ensure she could afford the ingredients she needed in order to make only her best desserts for the thousands who would be attending.

This was huge. H-U-G-E huge. But why her?

"Can I ask you something?"

Still on the other side of the counter from her, Brandon put down his fork and wiped his mouth with a napkin. "Shoot."

"Why are you doing all of this? I'm sure you could've found a more experienced chef or a more well-known bakery to partner with. Why us? Why me?"

"I already told you. I love your desserts."

"Come on."

"What can I say? I'm a sucker for pretty girls who can bake."

Months ago, she would've giggled at the compliment. Today, she shrugged it off. "I'm sure there are lots of prettier girls out there who can bake a lot better than I can. I'm serious. Tell me."

He raised an eyebrow. "I chose this bakery because I wanted more than just the same old deep fried ice cream and caramel *flan* on my menu. I wanted real, authentic desserts that reflected a true love for Latin food, but with a new modern twist. And I chose you, Ms. Robles, because you are as authentic as it gets."

"Wow. I don't know what to say. Thank you."

"You're welcome." He cleared his throat and pushed his empty plate to the side and threw his napkin on top of it. "Say, why don't you come to the restaurant tonight? We can celebrate our new partnership over dinner."

Part of her wanted to go. Maybe she did need a night off to forget her To Do list and forget Eric. It was a tempting offer, but it probably wasn't a good idea, given her recent emotional outbursts. She didn't trust herself out in public—or with other men—just yet.

"That sounds nice, but I'll have to take a rain check. I'm afraid I wouldn't be very good company. I'm a little distracted right now."

"Distracted? Or upset?"

"Why would you think I'm upset?"

"Amara, I'm barely thirty-years-old and I own two very successful restaurants. I didn't get to where I am without knowing how to read people and how to notice the little things…like, for instance, your red nose and sad eyes. Plus, I heard you crying when I came in."

Her cheeks burned. Imagining what Brandon must think of her now scraped her raw. She covered her mouth with her hand in an attempt to hide her quivering chin.

He reached over and pulled her hand down, his eyes full of concern—not pity. "Whoever he is, I'm sorry that he hurt you."

They stood there holding hands for several seconds. Why was he staring so intently at her? Why wasn't he letting go? Why wasn't she?

The hard slam of the back door made her jump and she broke free from his grasp.

"I'm sorry," he said, shaking his head. "I didn't mean to…I don't want you to think."

"It's okay." She gave him a quick smile as she heard Daisy approach.

"Hey, I'm here. What's going on?" Her cousin looked at her and then at Brandon.

"Brandon stopped by to drop off the rest of his deposit. And guess what? Because of him, the bakery is going to be part of the tasting event at this year's Southern California Food and Wine Festival! Isn't that amazing?"

Daisy shrieked, but quickly reined it back in. She gave Brandon a knowing smile. "Wow, that's awesome! Thanks Brandon. You're just always full of surprises, aren't you?"

Amara crooked her neck and gave her cousin a hard glare.

"No need to thank me. I'm just happy to help the bakery."

"And Amara, of course," said Daisy, the innuendo dripping from her lips like the caramel at the bottom of a flan custard. Amara kicked her cousin in the back of her shoe and Daisy stepped forward, hitting the counter with her waist.

Brandon didn't seem to notice. Instead, he gave her

cousin one of his charming smiles. "And you, Daisy."

Daisy raised her eyebrow at him and scoffed. "Me? How are you helping me, exactly?"

"Well, I heard you're starting to get more requests through the bakery to help out with parties. I know a lot of famous people, and famous people like to have parties, too. All I need are some business cards or fliers."

She laughed and waved him off. "I'm not a real party planner. I'm just helping out some of the bakery's longtime customers. This isn't something I'm going to do for a living."

Brandon shrugged. "Too bad. Amara told me you're in between jobs right now and this seems like the perfect opportunity for you to start your own your business. From what I've seen, you'd be really good at telling people what to do—you know—for their events."

Amara stifled a giggle. No one had ever called out Daisy like that. She looked at her cousin expecting a smart-ass remark, but Daisy just gaped at Brandon. Amara couldn't believe it.

"Okay then. I guess I better get going," Brandon finally said, after a few seconds of silence. He waved and turned toward the door.

She met Daisy's questioning eyes and mouthed, "What's wrong with you?"

"Oh, and Amara…" They both whipped their heads to look at Brandon, who was now holding open the front door. "That dinner invitation still stands. Just call me…when you're ready."

"I will. Thanks again."

Only when the door finally closed behind him did she look at Daisy. Her cousin pushed her left shoulder. "What the hell, Amara? Why did you tell Brandon that stuff about me?"

"What stuff? About not having a real job? He asked one day, and I told him you were rethinking your career choices. What's the big deal? He's a successful businessman and could teach us a few things."

"Well, judging by the way he was looking at you when I walked in, I think he's wanting to give you some private lessons. If you know what I mean."

Normally, Amara would dismiss any assumptions that a man like Brandon would be interested in her. But she couldn't deny the strange sensation she felt for those few seconds when they held hands.

"You know I'm right. That's why you're not denying it."

"No, I'm just not dignifying it with an answer. Besides, even if he did want something more, why are you so against it? Unless…"

Daisy threw up her hands. "I don't like him like that! I'm just trying to protect you, cousin. You're obviously heartbroken over Eric and I don't want anyone to take advantage of your condition."

The mention of Eric's name formed a lump in her throat. She swallowed any emotion and tried to sound normal. "Fine. Maybe I am sad about Eric leaving, but it's not like he promised me anything. And don't worry. Nothing will ever happen between me and Brandon because our business relationship is too important to me. Plus, I just don't think of him that way."

"Okay. Good. I'm sorry then for acting like such a brat."

"Does that mean you're going to think about what Brandon said? He has the connections, Daisy. He could really help."

"Maybe. I don't know. Just do me a favor and keep me out of your conversations, please. If he wants to know something about me, he can ask me directly."

"So, if he wants to know if you're single…?"

"Oh. My. God. Enough of trying to hook us up, okay? That's never going to happen."

Amara smiled. "Fine. I'll stop if you stop."

Daisy nodded and pushed Amara's shoulder again— softly this time. Amara pushed her back. "Thanks for looking out for me."

"Alright, that's enough of that," said Daisy. "Let's see what we've got to get done today."

As she watched her cousin flip through the order book, she blinked back tears. For all her talk about wanting to be independent and live her own life, it still felt nice to have someone in her corner who was prepared to throw down with anyone who threatened to hurt her. If Brandon was the business expert, then Daisy was the expert when it came to getting over a broken heart.

Hopefully, with both of their help, she'd survive the next few months intact.

• • •

The coldness of the house was the first thing he noticed.

As Eric wandered from room to room, he hugged himself tighter in attempt to warm up. Every room was empty now. Every room was bare. He'd just taken the last box out to the moving van and come back for…what?

One last check was what he'd told his mom. And

although there was nothing physical that they were leaving behind, he still felt a tug to check every cupboard and every closet. When he came up empty handed, Eric knew there was nothing left for him at this house. Only memories. And those he could take with him back to Vegas.

"It's all clear," he announced to his mom after walking back outside. She nodded and pulled down the van's back door. After dusting off her hands, she joined him as he waited for her by the driver's side door.

"You know I can still follow you there. The new project site doesn't open up until next week."

She put her hand on his arm. "We talked about this already. It's too much driving for you. Besides, I'm kind of looking forward to a road trip on my own. It'll be my first new adventure."

He nodded and watched her climb in behind the wheel.

"Have you talked to Amara?"

He widened his eyes. "Why are you asking?"

She shrugged and started up the van. "I don't know. I guess a part of me is hoping you were wrong about her—the way I was wrong about you."

"Well, to be fair, you weren't technically wrong about me. I did a lot of stupid things and you had every reason to think the way you did."

"Well, to be fair, I wasn't exactly winning any Best Mom prizes. I know I also did a lot of stupid things when you were younger. And you didn't deserve that. I hate that it took for your *abuela* to die to make me realize all the time we wasted. I want Amara and you to realize that every minute, every precious minute, is a gift. And if you want to be together, then you should do everything in your power to be together."

"See, but that's the thing, Mom. I don't think she wants us to be together. Or if she does, then she's too afraid to make it happen. And I can't want it for the both of us."

"How'd you get to be so wise about love?"

He looked at his *abuela*'s house one last time. "I guess I had a pretty good teacher."

His mom nodded, promised she'd call him every few hours, and then drove away, leaving him and his truck in the driveway. Just as he was about to get inside, a black Jeep pulled in behind him. It was Daisy.

She waved to him from the window and he walked over to her.

"Hey. What's up?"

"I came to give you this," she said, and handed him a flyer. It was the announcement of the bakery's grand re-opening on Friday.

Pride swelled inside him. She'd done it. She'd made her dream happen. He'd always imagined himself standing right next to her when it did. But that spot wasn't reserved for him anymore. Maybe it never was. "Thanks," he told Daisy, "but I don't think I can go. I'll probably be on my way to Vegas by then. Besides, I don't think Amara wants me there. Does she even know you're giving me this?"

"What does it matter? You miss her don't you?"

Of course he missed her. Cold showers and his other usual methods of relief hadn't helped him forget her. Because he didn't just miss having sex with Amara, he missed talking to her and laughing with her and just feeling her body next to his. Part of him had hoped that she would have called him that night to tell him she'd changed her mind and wanted him to stay. But she never did, and he didn't bother to pick up the phone either. And now it was too late. He looked at the ground, afraid Daisy would see the emotion he'd been trying to stifle ever since.

"So what happened between you two anyway?"

He jerked his head up to look at her. "What did she tell you?"

"Nothing. Absolutely nothing. But apparently *something* happened between you two and I wanna know what you plan on doing about it?"

"Look, Daisy. I care about her. I really do. And it's killing me that things didn't turn out differently. But whatever we had is over now."

"If you care so much about her, why are you leaving?"

He sighed. "Because it wouldn't have worked out. All the hiding and sneaking around isn't exactly the best way to have a relationship. We didn't want it to become this big thing between us and her parents, or me and Miguel."

"What do they have to do with it?"

"You know her parents can't stand me. Do you think they'd ever have let her take over the bakery if we started dating?"

"I don't know. Maybe."

"And then there's Miguel. He recommended me for the remodel, but only if I first swore to stay away from Amara. If I stay here in L.A. to be with her, then I can kiss any other job referrals from him and Amara's dad good-bye. And how can I be with Amara if I don't have a job? She needs someone to support her, not someone she's going to have to support financially. Trust me, it's better for everyone that we didn't stay together. Even us."

"Maybe you're right. Maybe everyone else is the reason you shouldn't be together. But if you ask me—okay, even if you don't ask me—I think that a part of you won't let yourself be with her either. At least not completely."

"That doesn't make any sense. I *was* with her."

"Maybe your body was. But, what about your heart? Did you ever tell her that you love her?"

Eric tensed. "How did you know?"

"You just told me. So, did you ever tell her?"

"It wouldn't have made a difference."

"You don't know that."

He shook his head. "I'm not the type of guy Amara needs in her life right now. She needs someone like Brandon." He practically spat the man's name.

"If I've learned anything about my cousin in these last few months is that she doesn't like other people deciding what she needs or doesn't need. *Especially* when it comes to men." She grimaced. "Maybe it's time for all of us to let Amara have a say in her own life."

"When she didn't ask me to stay, that was her having her say." He handed the flyer back to her. "Thanks for the invite, Daisy. But I won't be needing it."

She opened her mouth as if to say something else, but then closed it. Instead, she backed her Jeep out of the driveway.

Eric stood there for a few minutes. He knew Daisy had only tried to help. But talking about Amara and the way things ended between them was not how he wanted to spend his last day at his *abuela's* house. It was painful enough knowing that he'd never walk through that front door again and smell her hearty, rich *cocido*. And it was just as painful to be reminded that one of her dying wishes was for him to be with Amara, and he couldn't even do that right.

East Los Angeles had been his home. Now, all he wanted to do was get the hell out of it.

Time to start over. Again.

Chapter Twenty-One

As she surveyed the line of people that snaked out the door and onto the sidewalk, only one thought ran through Amara's head.

I'm going to wake up now. I'm going to wake up now. I'm going to wake up now.

The response to her Friday giveaway of two free pastries or bread items with every cup of coffee was overwhelming. For the first time since she could remember, there were people waiting outside before the bakery opened at six. The crowd was still going strong into the lunch hour and Amara couldn't believe that it wasn't just a very nice dream.

Day one of the bakery's weekend grand re-opening event was proving to be a great success. Today was about bringing in the college students and faculty by encouraging them to try their new menu of café lattes, cappuccinos, espressos, *cafes con leche,* and spiced hot chocolate. Tomorrow was about bringing in the community by offering special deals on breads and pastries and entertaining them with a mariachi trio in the morning.

Reinforcements had been called in. Daisy helped customers at the counter along with Trina, who was carrying little Miguel in one of those front backpack things. Mom ran the register, while her dad and brother helped by cleaning tables and folding boxes as needed.

Taking one last look at the beautiful craziness before her, Amara headed back to the kitchen to get started packing up a big order of *churros*

"Dad, I need your help," she yelled while she pulled two baking sheets from the oven. "Grab me some pastry boxes from the counter and help me pack up these *churros* for Fr. Marcos." Her hands full, she used one foot to lift the oven door about halfway up and then turned around and pushed it closed with her butt.

"Careful now. I'd hate to see that beautiful ass get burned."

Amara nearly dropped her trays at seeing Eric standing in the doorway holding a mini-tower of pastry boxes. She recovered her balance and set them on the stove. Determined not to show the volcano of emotions erupting inside at the sight of him, Amara took the boxes from his hands and headed back to the counter by the ovens.

"Are you going to say anything to me?" he asked.

She took a spatula from a nearby drawer. Her hand shook as she lifted one of the baked desserts off the baking sheet to place it into an empty box. "What are you doing here?" she finally managed.

He cleared his throat. "It looks like the grand re-opening is going well. Congratulations. And the front of the bakery looks awesome. The display cabinets really make a difference. Everything looks really, really good."

The deepness of his voice on that last sentence made goose bumps dance up and down her arms. Remembering that her dignity and fragile heart were at stake, she shook off the tremors and went back to packing the *churros*. "You didn't answer me. Why are you here? Why are you back?"

"Daisy stopped by the other day to drop off an invitation. She also told me I had some unfinished business here that I needed to take care of right away."

Ah, he came back to install the blinds. Daisy had mentioned to her yesterday that the old ones were starting to crack and that Amara should get someone to fix them. She closed her eyes and ordered her heart not to sink. She was too busy arguing with her emotions that she didn't notice when he moved behind her. Very close behind her.

"I was supposed to leave for Vegas yesterday. I had everything packed up in my truck, I closed out my bill at the motel I've been staying at, I even stopped at that corner liquor store to stock up on snacks for the road."

His breath caressed the back of her neck and she shivered. "So what are you doing here then?"

"I walked up to the counter to pay for my bottled waters and sunflower seeds and Mr. Veracruz, the owner, recognized me. He told me I owed him a hundred dollars. So, naturally, I think he's crazy and I show him that I'm only buying a couple of waters and the sunflower seeds. He tells me I owe him a hundred dollars for everything I used to steal from him back when I was in high school."

"So what did you do?"

"I gave him the hundred dollars, because I don't want

to be that guy anymore—the guy who doesn't pay for what he takes. Just like I don't want to be the guy who disappears when things get too hard." His breath turned hot against her exposed neck. "So I came back to finish what I started. I'm just hoping it's not too late."

She froze, leaving one *churro* in mid-lift. His arm came around her and he covered her hand holding the spatula. After gently pushing it down and returning the *churro* back to the baking sheet, he touched her bare shoulder. The skin-on-skin contact set off a whole new set of goose bumps. Her already slippery grip on the situation threatened to disintegrate. Before she turned around and got lost in those killer eyes, Amara needed to know for sure why he'd come back.

"Why are you here, Eric?" She whispered the words, yet the impact behind them was deafening.

"Because I love you, and someone tells me there's a very good chance you might just love me, too."

At first, she didn't move. She couldn't believe—wouldn't *let* herself believe—him. The magnitude of what he'd said… She started to tremble. It began with her knees and traveled up to her shoulders until she could do nothing but shake her head. She shrugged out of his half embrace and whipped around to face him.

"Is that what Daisy told you? I'm going to kill her. No, she's family. I can't kill her. I'll just injure her. Severely. Everyone needs to stop butting into my life. But they just can't help themselves. It's like a disease—"

"Amara, stop. I just told you that I loved you. Don't you have anything to say about that?"

Old insecurities washed over her. He loved her now but that didn't mean one day he wouldn't anymore. And then what? If she began a relationship with Eric, there was a good chance her parents would never sell her the bakery. Thanks to the success of the grand re-opening, she'd planned to bring it up again after this weekend.

Everything she'd ever wanted was within her grasp. Question was, what if she couldn't have both?

"Well?" Eric pressed again.

Amara's mind was a jumbled mess. Everything was moving so fast. Just a few minutes ago, she'd thought Eric had already left for Vegas. The fact that he was standing in front of her, professing his love, overwhelmed her. She couldn't form a coherent thought, let alone speak.

He took her silence for rejection.

"I guess Daisy was wrong, then. And so was I." He backed away, his gaze downcast. "Congrats on the grand re-opening, Amara. I won't bother you again."

It took her a few seconds to realize that Eric was walking away from her. It took her a few more seconds to realize that this time would be the last. He'd given her so many chances to admit how she felt, and now she was about throw away another one.

Because while she'd been so busy trying not to fall in love with Eric, she'd gone and fallen in love with Eric.

But if you tell him now, everyone will know.

And that's when it hit her. Oh. My. Gosh. She *wanted* everyone to know.

Amara ran through the kitchen and through the new shutter doors Eric had installed to separate it from the front of the bakery. It was filled with wall-to-wall customers and she searched the crowd for Eric. But he was nowhere to be seen. Her heart deflated. It was too late.

Jingle. Jingle.

She looked up and saw a black baseball cap about to head out the front door. She knew that baseball cap.

"Eric!" she shouted over the crowd. "Wait! I love you, too!"

The baseball cap stopped. Eric turned around and their eyes met.

"Amara, what are you doing?" Her mother's words were nearly drowned out by the rumble of the crowd, the things people must be saying about her, about him.

Good thing she didn't care anymore.

She walked toward him and Eric met her in the middle of the bakery. "Is that your new marketing strategy or something? Telling customers that you love them so they'll buy more cookies?"

"I have to admit that I'd do almost anything to sell more cookies. But you're the only customer I'll ever say that to."

The huge grin on his face was the last thing she saw before she pulled him down for a kiss. Gasps and claps sputtered from the crowd. She ignored them all and concentrated on the way Eric's lips were setting her entire body on fire.

"Okay, okay. Let's leave the lovebirds alone and get back to business. Who's next?" she heard Daisy yell. She smiled against his lips before pulling away from him at last. Then she took Eric by the hand and led him back into the kitchen.

Of course, they were followed.

"But I was in the middle of eating that cupcake, Consuelo!" her dad yelled as he barreled through the new shutter doors.

"*Basta*! Your daughter talking crazy is more important

than some cupcake. There she is! Talk some sense into her!"

"Amara, please tell your mother that you're not really in love with Eric Valencia so I can go get another cupcake before they are all gone."

"I'm sorry Dad, but I can't do that. I love Eric." She looked at him and smiled. He put his arm around her waist and pulled her to his side.

Consuelo gasped. "*Aye madre de dios.* You cannot, Amara! I forbid it!"

"I'm a grown woman, Mom. I can love whomever I want."

"But Amara, he's…"

"He's what? A man who worked his butt off to get this bakery ready, not because of the money, but because he believed in me and he wanted to make his *abuela* proud!" She knew she was yelling but she didn't care anymore who heard. "Yes, he made mistakes when he was a teenager, but that's not the man he is today. Any woman would be lucky to have him."

Even beneath the layers of her mother's Estee Lauder makeup, Amara could see the color draining from her face. Consuelo wrung her hands as if they were dishtowels.

Miguel pushed through the doors and went straight to Eric. "Dude, what happened to our agreement?"

"What agreement?" she looked at her brother and then back at Eric.

He pulled her tighter against him. "I know I promised you that I'd stay away from her, and I'm sorry that I broke that promise. But I'm not sorry that I fell in love with your sister. And if that's going to be a problem, then you'll just have to find a way to deal with it."

This gasp from her mother was louder than the first and her dad's mouth hit the floor. "Why are you both talking this way?" he asked after regaining his composure. "I'm so confused."

"I'm sorry, Mom and Dad, that you had to find out this way. But we've been seeing each other for a while and, yes, I hid it from you because I knew how you'd react. Just like I knew how you'd react when I tried to convince you to sell me the bakery. But I'm not afraid anymore to tell you how I feel about Eric, and I'm not afraid to tell you that things have to change around here. I need you to listen to me more."

"I'm still confused, *mija*. Things did change. We have a bakery full of new customers because we listened to you."

"I know, Dad. But it's not enough." She took a deep breath and forced herself to look at them both. "This bakery has been your whole life. The reason it's still open today is because of you and Mom. You should be proud of everything you've built here. But now it's time to let go—of the bakery and of me."

She waited for the interruption—the argument that she wasn't ready. That *they* weren't ready. But it never came. So she took another breath. No more holding back. No more biting her lip. It was time to tell them everything. "Today was a success and I know tomorrow will be, too. And so will next week and the week after. Remember, how I told you that I wanted you to believe in me? Well, now it's my turn. I really think I can take over the bakery full-time. I want you to sell it to me next year and retire."

"No, it's too much for you." Her dad rubbed his balding head—a sure sign he was torn.

"Maybe, but I can handle it. I can also handle living on

my own." She decided she might as well just rip the whole Band-Aid off at once. "I'm moving out. Miguel is going to help me renovate the storage area upstairs and turn it into a studio apartment."

"I am?" Her brother stared at her like she was talking crazy. She was. And it felt awesome.

"Are we that awful to live with that you'd rather live in a closet?" Her mother's voice sounded like she was on the verge of breaking down.

"I just need my own space, Mom. And I really need you—all of you," she said while glaring at her brother, "to stop butting into my personal business. No more telling me who I can or can't date."

"It's just that we want you to be happy," her mom whimpered.

"If you really want me to be happy, then you'll let me take over the bakery for real. You know it's time. You're grandparents now. You should be traveling and babysitting and doing all the other things you could never do while we were growing up because you had to run the bakery and raise us. It's time to start living the rest of your life, and it's time for me to start living mine."

Her dad took a step toward her. "Is this what you really want, Amara?"

Her eyes watered. Besides Eric, no one else had ever asked her that question. "Yes, Daddy, it is."

"Then it's yours." Her dad looked at her mom and she nodded then burst into tears.

The door to the kitchen swung open and Daisy barreled in with her hands up in the air. "What's going on in here? I'm running out of everything? Why is everyone crying?"

she yelled as she looked around the room.

Amara laughed through her tears. "My parents are retiring and I'm going to buy the bakery."

"That's awesome. Now, can everyone can back to work?" Daisy took a tray of pineapple *besos* and walked out.

"Since when did she become so bossy?" Amara's mom asked.

She laughed and reached for Eric's hand. He grabbed hers and held on tight.

"Okay, Mom and Dad, let's go," Miguel said, after clearing his throat. "I think Eric and Amara can handle things in here while we help Daisy out front."

To his credit, Eric waited about five seconds after they'd left before pulling her against him. His lips claimed hers in a hungry kiss that sedated her crazy rambling. Already starved for the taste of him, she kissed him back with equal force, sucking greedily on his lips and tongue. He groaned when she held his face in both of her hands, and then lifted her up onto the edge of the counter. Her legs wrapped around him and he moved his lips to her neck and collarbone.

"Tell me what you want," he whispered.

"I want you. I've always wanted you. I've always loved you," she whispered back.

"You drive me crazy, Amara Maria Robles," he said against her skin. "You make me want to do very bad things. Like take you right here in the middle of this kitchen."

She laughed and brought his head up so she could kiss his lips again. "I never knew bad boys could be corrupted by good girls."

He stopped his kisses to stare at her. "When they love them as much as I love you, they can. You make me want to be a better man."

She smiled and touched his cheek. "You don't need to change anything for me, Eric. I love the man you already are, the man that's holding me in his arms right here, right now."

He grinned and put his forehead against hers. What she saw in his dark, beautiful eyes filled her heart. She knew there would be no more pretending about who they thought they should be, no more letting others define who they were together. None of that mattered anymore.

Because when she looked into his eyes, she didn't see good or bad. She just saw forever.

Acknowledgments

As the saying goes, it takes a village. And this book would not exist if weren't for some very important and amazing people in my life. I'm definitely blessed.

First and foremost, to my own personal cheerleading squad: Louisa Bacio, Nikki Prince and Elizabeth Scott—I sincerely believe this book would've never been finished or submitted without your words of encouragement and gentle nudges. Thank you for being my friends and for inspiring me every day.

To Heather Howland for believing in this book even though she'd never tasted, let alone heard of, some of the Mexican desserts I wrote about. Thank you also for all of your expert notes, comments and edits which helped the story of Eric and Amara become more than I ever dreamed possible.

To the rest of my friends at OCC RWA, thank you for the constant support and for putting up with my blubbering speech when I got my roses for this book series' contract. I'm so grateful to be a part of this amazing group of writers.

To those crazy author types who belong to the Facebook Night Writers group, thanks for all of the midnight writing sprints that helped me get this book done.

To Rebecca Flenniken, Valentine Greiner, Tasha Henderson and Deanna Mora, thanks for reading this book before anyone else and letting me know what you loved and what I needed to work on. Your feedback was invaluable.

To my parents and the rest of my family, thank you for instilling in me a sense of pride for our Mexican heritage and for teaching me to share that with my children. Also, I blame my love/addiction for *pan dulce* on you.

To my three kids, for being proud of me even though you're not allowed to read my books and for understanding when I need to lock myself away in order to write.

And, finally, to my husband Patrick: Thank you for everything you do so I can fulfill my dream of being an author. This means nothing without your love and support. You and the kids are my world.

Te amo. Forever.

About the Author

Sabrina Sol is the *chica* who loves love. She writes steamy romance stories featuring smart and sexy Latina heroines. Sabrina lives in sunny Southern California with her husband, three kids, two Beagles and is part of a larger, extended Mexican family whose members are definitely *not* the source of inspiration for some of her characters. At least, that's what she's been telling them.

CPSIA information can be obtained
at www.ICGtesting.com
Printed in the USA
LVHW110705080221
678625LV00012B/459